M\
ROBERT WEINBERG

RAVES FOR THE SIDNEY TAINE ADVENTURE,
The Black Lodge

"A fine entertainment."

– Robert Bloch, author of *Psycho*

"Scary, witty, suspenseful, and fascinating. *The Black Lodge* is both a detective novel set on the seamy streets of Chicago, and a roller coaster ride of horror and mystery... The kind of horror novel I love – taut prose combined with a journey through the dark, occult country of fear... One of the top dark fantasies of the year."

– Douglas Clegg, author of *Neverland* and *Afterlife*

"Great fun – exciting, vivid, full of swift action, astonishing surprises, and a fascinating occult lore. I defy any reader to walk away from it after the first chilling encounter...."

– Hugh B. Cave, author of *Long Live the Dead: Tales from Black Mask*

PRAISE FOR *The Science of Superheroes*

"I found this book to be a hoot from beginning to end. Ms. Gresh and Mr. Weinberg must have spent some time in institutions for the deranged, because well-balanced minds could not have conceived of this project. But thank God for their derangement, for they have produced a package of pure fun from first page to last. If, like me, you admire superheroes from a distance, or if you are a hardcore fan of them, you will enjoy this book as surely as you would enjoy waking one morning to discover that you are invincible, able to fly, and in possession of a totally cool costume behind which to hide your true identity."

> – Dean Koontz, from the introduction
> of *The Science of Superheroes*

DEMONIC DELIGHTS DEALT IN *The Devil's Auction*

"I haven't had this much fun since I beat my pet hamster to death with a chair leg! A rootin-tootin booger of a book! Fresh as a spring daisy, but mean and nasty as a rattlesnake bite!"

> – Joe R. Lansdale, author of *Mucho Mojo*
> and *Bubba Ho-Tep*

"Marvelous!"

> – Philip José Farmer, author of the ground-breaking
> *Riverworld* series

SUSPENSEFUL SATISFACTION GUARANTEED BY *A Logical Magician*

"Alternately suspenseful and hilarious... The most satisfying fantasy I have read in a long time."

> – L. Sprague de Camp, author of *Lest Darkness Fall* and
> *The Complete Enchanter* (with Fletcher Pratt)

"Entertaining... lighthearted... a lot of fun."

> – Charles De Lint in *Mystery Scene*

Rollicking Glee for *A Calculated Magic*

"There are few writers who can consistently combine the mundane with sheer fantasy and produce a work acceptable to both logic and imagination. Mr. Weinberg, having successfully done this once in *A Modern Magician*, now produces a very worthy sequel."
— Andre Norton, author of *Dragon Blade: The Book of the Rowan* (Cycle of Oak, Yew, Ash, and Rowan)

"The book is fun, which to my way of thinking is the main reason for reading fiction in the first place."
— L. Sprague de Camp, author of *Lest Darkness Fall* and *The Complete Enchanter* (with Fletcher Pratt)

"Remember those old amusement park rides where you sat in a boat and were carried along through a dark, spooky tunnel with all sorts of fantasy figures leaping up in flashing lights to scare you half to death? *A Calculated Magic* is such a ride, except that Robert Weinberg's boat is a speedboat at full throttle. This is a pleasure cruise you'll be telling your friends about!"
— Hugh B. Cave, Author of *Legion of the Dead*

"It's difficult to balance humor and suspense in the same story but Weinberg manages the job rather neatly, alternating wisecracks with tense situations and hectic action."
— *Science Fiction Chronicle*

"I was captivated."
— Robert Bloch, author of *Psycho*

BOOKS BY ROBERT WEINBERG

Sidney Taine is also featured in *The Black Lodge* (novel)
Ms. Sydney Taine is also featured in *Nightside 1-4*
(Marvel comic book series)

Horror Novels
The Devil's Auction
The Black Lodge
The Dead Man's Kiss
The Armageddon Box

Humorous Fantasy Novels
A Logical Magician (released in England as *A Modern Magician*)
A Calculated Magic

World of Darkness Novels
Vampire Diary: The Embrace (with Mark Rein*Hagen)
The Machiavelli Conundrum (graphic novel from Moonstone Comics)

WOD: MASQUERADE OF THE RED DEATH TRILOGY
Blood War
Unholy Allies
The Unbeholden

WOD: THE HORIZON WAR TRILOGY
The Road to Hell
The Ascension Warrior
War in Heaven

Techno Thriller
The Termination Node (with Lois H. Gresh)

Dark Earth Novel
Dark Earth - The Torch (Berkley Books, forthcoming)

City of Heroes Novel
The Web of Arachnos (forthcoming, CDS books, October 2005)

Short Story Collections
Dial Your Dreams
The Occult Detective
The Complete Morgan Smith (forthcoming, e-book, 2006)

Non-Fiction Books
The Hero Pulp Index (with Lohr McKinstry)
The Revised Hero Pulp Index (completely revised by RW in 1972)
WT50
The Man Behind Doc Savage
The Weird Tales Story
The Annotated Guide to Robert E. Howard's Swords and Sorcery
A Biographical Dictionary of SF/Fantasy Artists
The Louis L'Amour Companion
The Computers of Star Trek (with Lois H. Gresh)
Horror of the 20th Century
The Science of Superheroes (with Lois H. Gresh)
The Science of Supervillains (with Lois H. Gresh)
The Science of Anime (with Lois H. Gresh, forthcoming, Dec. 2005)
The Science of James Bond (with Lois H. Gresh, forthcoming, April 2006)

Comic Books
Cable 79-96 (Marvel)
Nightside 1-4 (Marvel)
Extinction Event 1-5 (Wildstorm/DC)
Vampire: The Machiavelli Conundrum (Moonstone)
World's End (with Scott Lobdell, Chris Claremont, Marvel Graphic novel)

Twilight Tales presents...

THE OCCULT DETECTIVE

By
ROBERT WEINBERG

Twilight Tales presents... THE OCCULT DETECTIVE

Twilight Tales

DEDICATION

To Tina -

the original black magic woman!

Zowie!

CONTENTS

INTRODUCTION:
PLAIN TAINE

The landscape of modern horror fiction is so overpopulated with occult detectives that you would need to hire one to find another with even a smidgen of originality. These days, it seems, just about everybody is hanging out a shingle proclaiming their skill at solving befuddling mysteries steeped in the supernatural. Just look at the variety of sleuths from the last two decades alone who have brought their knowledge of the occult to bear against seemingly uncanny menaces: high school cheerleaders, clinical pathologists, private eyes with one foot in the darkside, greasy-spoon waitresses, psychologically and physically challenged sleuths, alternate world enforcers, werewolves who like to sink their teeth into crime-solving, newspaper reporters, secret agents who know the damning truth is *out there*, detectives who didn't know they were ghosts (eeek!), even soccer moms who try to keep their black magic paraphernalia hidden from hubby and the kids. A short time ago vampire detectives were all the rage – now there's more of them on the street every night than there are perps. About the only psychic detective we haven't seen yet is a zombie detective on a low-salt diet (but just wait).

This is all good fun, of course, and it has helped to broaden the horizons of the horror tale as much as any variations on one of its popular themes could. But it does suggest that the psychic detective – an iconic figure in weird fiction whose history extends back to the middle of the nineteenth century – is just the latest trend to catch the fancy of horror genre wannabes. With so many psychic sleuths competing for clients and cases, it's inevitable that all want to stand out from the herd. Most of their creators do this by tweaking the most superficial aspects of their characters. Have your detective speak in pidgin-French, and it distinguishes him from the dumb gumshoe who speaks plain English. Give your detective a wiseass demonic familiar and he (or she – another increasingly less original twist to make your tales original) automatically commands more attention than the mere mortal who follows police procedure by the book (or grimoire, if you will). And who do you think is more likely to be put on retainer busting ghosts and incarcerating incubi: the psychic dick who knows a sorcerer's spell or two, or the one with a gun that shoots *ectoplasm*?

Odds are, when you look through the facades of these "Why wear black when you can wear *sable*?" candidates, and check their resumes, they have little to show other than the usual run of spooky encounters: the haunted house that needs exorcising, the vampire that doesn't respond to the cross or stake, the demon that can be dispatched back to hell only by the person who knows the right invocation. *Ho-hum!* Are supernatural mysteries really this predictable?

If you're looking for an occult detective whose merits are measured by the unique cases he takes, the equally unique solutions they call for, and the entertaining tales they elaborate – then, dear reader, meet Sid Taine, psychic sleuth extraordinaire. He's a back-to-basics guy cut from the mold of the classic American detective: hard-working, skilled with the tools of his trade, and respected for his principles as well as his acumen. It's his ability to blend in with the scene, *not* to stand out from it, that gets him the interesting work.

It should come as no surprise that Sid Taine comes so highly recommended – or at the very least deserving of this book of his collected adventures. By the time he was imagined into being, his creator, Bob Weinberg, was a seasoned veteran with more than two decades of horror writing under his belt. Indeed, Bob already had two series occult investigators to his credit: Morgan Smith, a Robert E. Howard-style hero who grappled with Lovecraftian horrors in some two-dozen stories written for the specialty press magazines of the 1960s and '70s, and Alex Warner and Valerie Lancaster, a scholarly duo who went to the mat with weird menaces in the novels *The Devil's Auction* and *The Armageddon Box*. Think of Sid Taine as a distillation of the best aspects of these very different characters and their series: he's a detective with a swashbuckler's flair for attracting danger, and he always brings intelligence and grace to his devilish encounters.

Another reason why Taine seems so good at what he does is a little more speculative. Taine shares a last name with John Taine, a writer of science fiction stories in the first half of the twentieth century. In "real life," Taine was Eric Temple Bell, a distinguished mathematician whose academic brilliance was reflected in the intriguing speculations he wove into his blends of mystery, adventure, and fantastic fiction. In his *former* life, Bob Weinberg took a degree in mathematics at Stevens Institute of Technology in Hoboken, New Jersey (about the same time that he was penning his Morgan Smith tales). It might be a stretch to suggest that Sid Taine is Bob Weinberg's fiction alter ego, but it's hard not to think of Bob when Taine quotes *sotto voce* some squib from a classic horror story, or when his adventures evoke a horror plot that only someone as well read as Bob is in horror fiction would know. (Did I mention that Bob also collects John Taine novels?)

Of course you wouldn't know all this about Sid Taine just by looking at him. He's about as unassuming in appearance as detectives come, and about as unremarkable as anyone who traffics regularly with the supernatural can get – at least on the surface. Here's the thumbnail sketch of him provided for his first appearance in *The Black Lodge*, his only novel-length adventure (and the only Sid Taine story not reprinted in this book, more's the pity):

> "Thirty-one years old, male, Caucasian. Six feet, two inches tall; weight, two hundred and fourteen pounds. No scars or distinguishing characteristics. Taine runs a private investigation agency from Chicago's Acme Building on the North Side. His one employee, Mary McConnell, serves as both secretary and researcher."

Taine has earned the nickname "The New Age Detective" from his use of harmonic frequencies, crystals and other occult paraphernalia, but you never really see him fiddle with those. In private, he does a tarot reading before embarking on a case – the equivalent of a private detective checking to make sure his gun is loaded and that his back-up clip is full. He's not a gimmick guy who goes around spouting supernatural mumbo-jumbo or working the flashy sleight-of-hand that makes clients and monsters alike go "oooohh!" He's a results guy: most of his early assignments are missing-persons cases (what made the persons missing is usually the challenge of the mystery), and his success rate is an unheard of 90 percent.

Compare the first story in this book to the last and you'll find that Sid Taine hasn't changed much in the last 15 years. He still has the same look. He still works the same Chicago beat (although his cases may eventually take him overseas and to stranger places). He still flirts occasionally with the female clients whose lives he saves (but he always maintains his professional detachment). If he were a gunslinger, the only difference you might notice is a few more notches on the handle of his pistol.

But what Bob Weinberg doesn't lavish on Sid Taine in the way of character details or superficial accoutrement he more than invests in the plotting and conceptualization of his adventures. These stories are high-water marks in Bob's body of work as a horror writer, and their ingenuity sticks in your mind long after tales of other psychic sleuth slackers have faded.

The Black Lodge, like all of Bob's novels, is a gem of intricate plotting in which disparate subplots involving urban and white collar crime intersect under the influence of an all pervasive supernatural menace. If Bob excels at anything as a storyteller, it's in persuading the reader that there are occult machinations behind the most inconsequential and seemingly unrelated events: dip into this book and you'll quickly become a devout supernatural conspiracy theorist. In this story, Taine immediately stands apart from other detectives of his ilk because of the threat to life and limb he faces. Far too many occult detective stories fall flat because the hero, armed with his overwhelming knowledge of the Unknown, never once doubts his invincibility and so never once invites the reader's sympathy. Not Sid Taine – in nearly every one of his adventures his life is imperiled by the horrors he faces. They're inevitably a supernatural streetfight to the death, and the reader feels, with Taine, their every blow.

"Terror in the Night" is a valentine of sorts to fans of horror fiction. Taine evokes H.P. Lovecraft and his fiction in an amusing throwaway comment, but the story will resonate with readers who are also familiar with the work of Edward Lucas White and Henry S. Whitehead. How many psychic detective stories have you read where the hero's familiarity with ideas treated in horror fiction is crucial to solving the mystery? (For those who wish to see Bob working that same idea in a different way, pick up his pair of anti-heroic comic fantasies, *A Logical Magician* and *A Calculated Magic*.)

It's hard picking favorites from the Taine oeuvre, but if pinned down I would have to designate "The Midnight El," with "The Apocalypse Quatrain" a close second. The first is a variation on a theme that usually shows up in fantasy fiction as the deal-with-the-devil story in which the protagonist must find some legitimate way to outwit old Scratch. In the second, Taine puts on the gloves to go a few rounds with the dreadful implications of a prophecy of Nostradamus. Like fair-play mysteries, these stories feed readers all the clues they need to race the detective to the solution. Both are unusual for their use of logic (see – there's Bob's math background again) as part of the occult detective's armamentarium.

Logic also plays a role in "Seven Drops of Blood," but in a completely unforeseeable way. It was Raymond Chandler who drew the comparison between the modern detective and the knights of yore, so leave it to Sid Taine to give this detective caper a spin into Camelot territory. The story makes a diptych of sorts with "The Children of May," another Taine tale with an Arthurian slant. It's worth pointing out that both of these stories were written especially for anthologies with Arthurian themes. You wouldn't guess it by how well they fit the regular Taine canon.

If, as these stories suggest, Taine is like a knight pure of heart, then it's easy to see him fitting the heroic form molded from medieval legend and reinterpreted in modern times through comic book superhero scenarios. Hence the foundation of "Enter, the Eradicator!" where we find out something interesting about Taine's personal life: he's got a sister, Sydney, with an extradimensional pedigree, who works as a detective herself in an alternate New York City. Bob created Sydney for the four-part story "Ikkyu's Skull" that appeared as part of Marvel Comics Nightside series between 2001 and 2002. Pick up a set of the comics today, read about Sydney's run-in with Arkady Dread and the Black Dragon Society, and you'll see why she's so well-equipped to navigate the superhero universe as she does here. (You'll also want to see Tom Derenick's depiction of Sid, who makes a cameo appearance in one of the panels.) If you didn't know that Bob wrote alternate-world horror thrillers for White Wolf's Masquerade of the Red Death and Horizon War series, and if you didn't know about Bob's acclaimed work in comics, notably his writing for the X-Men line, then this story makes a perfect bridge.

Until recently, only a few of the Sid Taine stories had been collected. This volume makes the most comprehensive dossier to date of one of weird fiction's most unpredictable crime-stoppers. That's good news for all readers, whether you're a hardcore fan of Bob's (or is that Sid's?) or coming to these tales new. Look out ghosts, ghouls, and other denizens of the dark side: Sid Taine is on the case, and soon to be on yours.

–*Stefan Dziemianowicz*
New York, 2005

THE MIDNIGHT EL

Cold and alone, Sidney Taine waited for the Midnight El. Collar pulled up close around his neck, he shivered as the frigid Chicago wind attacked his exposed skin. With temperatures hovering only a few degrees above zero, the stiff breeze off Lake Michigan plunged the wind chill factor to twenty below. Not even the usual drunks haunted the outdoor subway platforms on nights like these. Fall asleep outside in the darkness and you never woke up.

Taine hated the cold. Though he had lived in Chicago for more than a year, he had yet to adjust to the winter weather. Originally from San Francisco, he delighted his hometown friends when he groused that he never realized what the phrase "chilled to the bone" meant until he moved to the Windy City.

A sly grin and dark, piercing eyes gave him a sardonic, slightly mysterious air. An image he strived to cultivate. Like his father and grandfather before him, Taine worked as a private investigator.

Though he had opened his office in Chicago only fourteen months ago, he was already well-known throughout the city. Dubbed by one of the major urban newspapers as "The New Age Detective," Taine used both conventional techniques and occult means to solve his cases. While his unusual methods caused a few raised eyebrows, no one mocked his success rate. Specializing in missing-person investigations, Taine rarely failed to locate his quarry. Although, he had his doubts about tonight's assignment.

Before leaving his office this evening, Taine had mixed, then drank, an elixir with astonishing properties. According to a famous grimoire, *The Key of Solomon*, the potion enabled the user to see the spirits of the dead. Its effects lasted until dawn, which was more than enough time for Taine. If he failed tonight, there would be no second chance.

The detective glanced down at his watch for the hundredth time. The glowing hands indicated five minutes to twelve. According to local legends, it was nearly the hour for the Midnight El to start its run.

No one knew how or when the stories began. A dozen specialists in urban folklore supplied the detective with an equal number of fabled origins. One and all, they were of the opinion that the tales dated back to the first decades of the century, when the subway first debuted in Chicago.

A few old timers, mostly retired railway conductors and engineers, claimed the Midnight El continued an even older tradition – the Phantom Train, sometimes called the Death's Head Locomotive. Despite the disagreements, several elements remained constant in all the accounts. The Midnight El hit the tracks exactly at the stroke of twelve. Its passengers consisted of those who had died that day in Chicago. The train traversed the entire city, starting at the station closest to the most deaths of the day, working its way along from there.

Taine waited on a far south side platform. Earlier in the day, twelve people had died in a flash fire only blocks from this location. There was little question this would be the train's first stop.

Slowly, the seconds ticked past. A harsh west wind wailed off the Lake, like some dread banshee warning Taine of his peril. With it came the doleful chiming of a distant church bell striking the hour. Midnight – the end of one day, start of another.

The huge train came hurtling along the track, rumbling like distant thunder. Emerging ghostlike out of thin air, dark and forbidding, blacker than the night, it lumbered into the station. Lights flashed red and yellow as it slowed to a stop.

Taine caught a hurried vision inside a half-dozen cars as they rumbled past. Pale, vacant, *dead* faces stared out into the night. Riders from another city, or another day, he wasn't sure which, and he had no desire to know. Young and old, black and white, men and women, all hungering for a glimpse of life.

Hissing loudly, double doors swung open on each car. A huge, shadowy figure clad in a conductor's uniform emerged from midway along the train. In his right hand he held a massive silver pocket watch, hooked by a glittering chain to his vest. Impatiently, he stood there, waiting for new arrivals.

The conductor's gaze swept the station, rested on Taine for a moment, then continued by. The ghost train with all its passengers was invisible to mortal eyes. There was no way for the conductor to know that the man on the platform could actually see him. Nor suspect what Taine planned to do.

Once, the conductor had been a ferryman; the ancient Greeks knew him as Charon. To the Egyptians, he had been Anubis, the Opener of the Way. A hundred other cultures named him a hundred different ways. But always his task remained the same: transporting the newly dead to their final destination.

They came with the wind. Not there, then suddenly there. Each one stopped to face the conductor for an instant before being allowed to pass. The breath froze in Taine's throat as he watched them file by. Those who had died that day.

His hands clenched into fists when he sighted three pajama-clad, black children. Today's newspapers had been filled with all the grisly details of the sudden tenement fire that had resulted in their deaths. None of them had been over six years old.

Wordlessly, the last of the three turned. Lonely, mournful eyes stared deep into Taine's for an instant. The detective remained motionless. If he reacted now, it might warn the conductor. An instant passed, and then the child and all the other passengers were gone. Disappeared into the Midnight El.

The conductor stepped back into the doorway. Raising one hand, he signaled *continue* to some unseen engineer. Seeing his chance, Taine acted.

Moving with the grace of a stalking tiger, the detective darted at, then around, the astonished doorman. Before the shadowy figure could react, Taine was past him and into the subway. Ignoring the restless dead on all sides, the detective headed for the front of the car.

"Come back here," commanded the conductor, stepping aboard. Behind him, the doors swung shut. An instant later, the car jerked forward as the engine came to life. Outside, scenery blurred as the train gained speed. The floor shook with a gentle, rocking motion. The Midnight El was off to its next stop.

Taine relaxed, letting his pursuer catch up to him. Surprise had enabled him to board the ghostly train. Getting off might not prove so easy.

"You do not belong on the Midnight El, Mr. Taine," said the conductor. He spoke calmly, without any trace of accent. Listening closely, Taine caught the barest hint of amusement in the phantom's voice. "At least, not yet. Your time is not for years and years."

"You know my name, and instant of my death?" asked Taine, not the least bit intimidated by the imposing bulk of the other. Six feet, four inches tall, weighing a bit more than two hundred and thirty pounds, Taine resembled a professional football player.

Surrounded by the shadows, the ticket taker towered over Taine by a head. His face, though human, appeared cut from weathered marble. Only his black, black eyes burned with life. "Past, present, future mean nothing to me. One look at a man is all I need to review his entire life history, from the moment of his birth to the last breath he takes. It's part of my job, supervising the Midnight El."

"For what employer?"

"Someday, you'll learn the answer," replied the conductor, with a chuckle. "But it won't matter much then." He reached into his vest pocket and pulled out the silver pocket watch. "Thirteen minutes to the next stop. This train, unlike most, always runs on time. You shall exit there, Mr. Taine."

"And if I choose not to?"

"You must." The conductor frowned. "I cannot harm you. Such action is strictly forbidden under the terms of my employment. However, I appeal to your sense of compassion. A living presence on this train upsets the other passengers. Think of the pain you are inflicting on them."

Darkness gathered around the railroad man. He no longer looked so human. His coal-black eyes burned with inhuman intensity. "Leave them to their rest, Mr. Taine. You do not belong here."

"Nor does one other."

The conductor sighed, his rock-hard features softening in sorrow. "I should have guessed. You came searching for Maria Hernandez. Why?"

"Her husband hired me. He read about my services in the newspapers. I'm the final resort for those who refuse to give up hope.

"Victor told me what little he knew. My knowledge of the occult filled in the blanks. Combined together, the facts led me here."

"All trails end at the Midnight El," declared the conductor, solemnly. "Though I'm surprised you realized that."

"It was the only possible solution. Maria disappeared three nights ago. Vanished without a trace off of an isolated underground subway platform exactly at midnight. No one else recognized the significance of the time.

"The police admitted they were completely baffled. The ticket seller remembered Maria taking the escalator down to the station a few minutes before twelve. A transit patrolman spoke to her afterwards. He remembered looking up at the clock and noting the lateness of the hour. But when he looked around, the woman was no longer there. Somehow, she disappeared in the blink of an eye. Searching the tunnels for her body turned up nothing."

Taine paused. "Victor Hernandez considered me his last and only chance. I promised him I would do my best. I never mentioned the Midnight El."

"My thanks to you for that," said the conductor, nodding his understanding. "Suicides cause me the greatest pain. Especially those who sacrifice themselves to join the one they love."

"She meant a great deal to him," said Taine. "They were only married a few months. It seemed quite unfair."

"The world is unfair," said the conductor, shrugging his massive shoulders. "Or so I have been told by my passengers. Again and again, for centuries beyond imagining."

"She wasn't dead. If I don't belong here, then neither does she."

The conductor grimaced. He looked down at his great silver watch and shook his head. "There's not enough time to explain. Our schedule is too tight for long talks. Please understand my position."

"The Greeks considered Charon the most honorable of the gods. Of course, that was a thousand years ago."

"Spare me the dramatics," said the conductor. A bitter smile crossed his lips. He nodded to himself, as if making an important decision. Slowly, ever so slowly, he twisted the stem on the top of his watch.

All motion ceased. The subway car no longer shook. Outside, the blurred features of the city solidified into grotesque shapes, faintly resembling the Chicago skyline.

Taine grunted in surprise. "You can stop time?"

"For a little while," said the conductor. "Don't forget, the Midnight El visits every station within the space of a single night. On a hot summer night in a violent city like this, we often need extra minutes for all the passengers. Thus my watch. Twisting a little more produces a timeless state."

"The scenery?" asked Taine, not wanting to waste his questions, but compelled by the alienness of the landscape to ask.

"All things exist in time as well as space. Take away that fourth dimension and the other three seem twisted."

The phantom conductor turned and beckoned with his other hand. "Maria Hernandez. Attend me."

A short, slender woman in her early twenties pushed her way forward through the ranks of the dead. Long brown hair, knotted in a single thick braid, dropped down her back almost to her waist. Wide, questioning eyes looked at the detective. Unlike all the others on the train, a spark of color still touched Maria's cheeks, and her chest rose and fell with her every breath.

"Tell Mr. Taine how you missed the subway two weeks ago," said the conductor. He glanced at Taine, as if checking to make sure the detective was paying attention.

"There was a shortage in one of the drawers at closing time," began Maria, her voice calm, controlled. "My superior asked me to do a cross-check. It was merely a mathematical error, but it took nearly twenty minutes to find. By then, I was ten minutes late for my train."

She hesitated, as if remembering something particularly painful. "I was in a hurry to get home. It was our six-month anniversary. When I left that morning for the bank, my husband, Victor, promised me a big surprise when I returned. I loved surprises."

"Yes, I know," said the conductor, his voice gentle. "He bought you tickets to the theater. But that is incidental to the story. Please continue."

"Usually, I have to wait a few minutes for my train. Not that night. It arrived exactly on schedule. When I reached the El platform, the conductor was signaling to close the doors. The next train wasn't for thirty minutes. So I ran. I would have made it, too, if it wasn't for my right heel." She looked down at her shoes. "It caught in a crack in the cement. Wedged there so tight I couldn't pull my foot loose. By the time I wrenched free, the train had already left."

"Two weeks ago," said Taine, comprehension dawning. "The day of the big subway crash in the Loop."

"Four minutes after Mrs. Hernandez missed her train, it crashed headlong into another, stalled on the tracks ahead," said the conductor. "Fourteen people died when several of the cars sandwiched together. *Fifteen* should have perished."

"Fate," said Taine.

"She was destined to die," replied the conductor, as if explaining the obvious. "It was woven in the threads. A mistake was made somewhere. Her heel should have missed that crack. There was probably a knot in the twine. I assure you her name was on my passenger list. Maria was scheduled to ride the Midnight El."

"So, when she didn't, you decided to correct that mistake on your own," said Taine, his temper rising. Mrs. Hernandez stood silent, as if frozen in place. Her story told, the conductor ignored her.

"I thought a living person on board disturbed the dead?"

"With effort, the rules can be bent," said the conductor. He sighed. "It grows so boring here. You cannot imagine how terribly boring. I desired company, someone to talk to. Someone alive, someone with feelings, emotions. The dead no longer care about anything.

"The Three Sisters had to unravel a whole section of the cloth. They needed to weave a new destiny for Mrs. Hernandez to cover up their mistake. Meanwhile, Maria should have been dead but was still alive. Her spirit belonged to neither plane of existence. It took no great effort to bring her on the train as a passenger. And, here she will remain, for all eternity, neither living or dead, but in a state between the two. Immortal, undying, unchanging – exactly like me. Forever."

Taine's fists clenched in anger. "Who gave you the power to decide her fate? That's not your job. You're only the ferryman, nothing more. She doesn't belong here. I won't allow you to do this."

"Your opinion means nothing to me, Mr. Taine." The conductor's left hand rested on the stem of the pocket watch. "There is nothing you can do to stop me."

"Like hell," said the detective, and leapt forward.

A powerfully built man, he moved with astonishing speed. Once tonight he had caught the conductor by surprise. This time, he did not.

The phantom's left hand shot out and caught Taine by the throat. Without effort, he raised the detective into the air, so that the man's feet dangled inches off the floor. "I am not fooled so easily a second time."

Taine flailed wildly with both hands. Not one of his punches connected. Desperately, the detective lashed out one foot, hitting the conductor in the chest. The phantom didn't even flinch.

"In my youth I wrestled with Atlas and Hercules. Your efforts pale before theirs, Mr. Taine."

Neither man nor spirit noticed Mrs. Hernandez cautiously reaching for the silver pocket watch the trainman held in his other hand. Not until she grabbed it away.

"What!" bellowed the conductor, dropping Taine and whirling about. "You…you…"

"Just because I obeyed your commands," said Mrs. Hernandez, "didn't mean I no longer possessed a will of my own. I was waiting for the right opportunity." She gestured with her head at the crowds of the dead all around them. "I'm not like them. I'm alive."

She held the pocket watch tightly, one hand on the stem. "If you try to take this away, I'll break it. Don't make me do that."

Taine, his throat and neck burning with pain, staggered to Mrs. Hernandez's side. "Let us go. Otherwise, we'll remain here forever, frozen in time."

"Nonsense," said the conductor. "I told you the rules can only be bent so far. Sooner or later, the strain will become too great and snap this train back to the real world."

"But, if Maria breaks your watch," said Taine, "what then? You admitted needing its powers. Think of the problems maintaining your schedule without it."

"True enough." The conductor paused for a moment, as

if in thought. "I am willing to offer this compromise. Maria cannot leave this train without my permission. The Fates will not spin her a new destiny as long as she remains on the El. Return the watch to me, and I'll give her a chance to return to her husband. And resume her life on Earth."

"A chance?" said the detective, suspiciously. "What exactly do you mean by that?"

"A gamble, a bet, a *wager*, Mr. Taine," said the conductor. "Relieve my boredom. Ask me a question, any question. If I cannot answer, you and Mrs. Hernandez go free. If I guess correctly, then both of you remain here for all eternity – not dead but no longer among the living – on the Midnight El. It will take a great deal of effort, but I can manage. Take it or leave it. I refuse to bend any further."

"Both of us?" said Taine. "You raised the stakes. And what about disturbing the dead? A little while ago you were anxious for me to leave."

"As I stated before, the rules can be bent. After all, I am the ferryman. And," continued Charon, the faintest trace of a smile on his lips, "what better way to sharpen your wits, Mr. Taine, than to put your own future at peril?"

"According to your earlier remarks, there's nothing in the world you don't know."

"There is only one omniscient presence. Man or spirit, we are mere reflections of his glory. Still," he added, as an afterthought, "the universe holds few mysteries for me."

Shadows gathered around the phantom. He extended one huge hand. "Make your decision. Now. Before I change my mind."

His eyes burned like two flaming coals. "No tricks. An answer must exist for your question."

"Give him the watch," Taine said to Maria.

"You agree?" asked the conductor.

"I agree," replied the detective, calmly.

The conductor twisted the stem of his great silver watch. Immediately, the scenery shifted, and the subway car started shaking.

"We arrive at the next station in a few minutes," Charon announced smugly. "You have until then to frame your question."

Maria gasped, raising her hands to her face. "But…that's cheating."

"Not true. I promised no specific length of time for our challenge." The conductor glanced down at his watch. "Your time is ticking by quickly. Better think fast."

Taine took a deep breath. Not all questions depended on facts for their answer. He prayed that the ferryman would not renege on their bargain once he realized his mistake. "You trapped yourself. I'm ready now."

"You are?" said the conductor, frowning.

"Are you prepared to accept defeat?"

"Impossible."

"Then tell me the answer to the question raised when I first boarded the train. When is the exact moment of my death?"

"You will perish…" began the conductor, then stopped, mouth open in astonishment. Slowly, the fire left his eyes. He shook his head. "Caught by my own words."

Maria Hernandez turned to Taine. "I don't understand. Caught? How?"

"The conductor bragged earlier that he knew the date of my death," said Taine. "If he answers correctly, then he wins our bet."

"And," continued Maria, comprehension dawning, "by the terms of the agreement, you must remain on the Midnight El forever."

"Thus making his prediction false," finished Taine, "since I cannot die when he predicts. On the other hand, if he says I will never die, then he does not know the date of my death. Which means he cannot answer the question. So, whatever he says, I am the winner. The bet is ours."

With a sigh, the conductor pocketed his watch. "You would have made good company, Mr. Taine."

Metal screeched on metal as the Midnight El pulled into

the next station. "This is your stop. Farewell."

They were alone on a deserted subway station with a cold wind blowing.

Tears filled Maria Hernandez's eyes. "Are we really free?"

Taine nodded, his thoughts drifting. Already, he searched for an explanation for Maria's disappearance that would satisfy both the police and her husband.

"As free as any man or woman can be," he answered somberly. "For in the end, we all have a date to keep with the Midnight El."

←----→

SEVEN DROPS OF BLOOD

-1-

"**I** want you to locate," said the man in dark glasses, his voice intent, "the Holy Grail."

Not sure how to reply, Sidney Taine stretched back in his chair and stared across the desk at his client. The speaker was a short, stocky man, impeccably dressed in a grey pinstripe suit and charcoal tie. His sharp, almost angular features appeared cut from solid rock. A full black beard covered most of his jaw. Heavy dark eyebrows flowed together above his glasses, giving his features a sinister turn. His wide nose jutted out from the center of his face like the sharp beak of some massive bird of prey. He looked and sounded like a man accustomed to getting his own way.

Ashmedai was the name he used; he had not indicated whether it was first or last or both. His smooth, confident motions entering Taine's office made it clear that the eyes behind the black lenses were not those of a blind man. What secret those glasses actually hid, the detective was not sure he wanted to learn. According to ancient Hebrew tradition, Ashmedai reigned as king of demons.

"I'm not King Arthur," said Taine slowly, measuring his reply. "Nor am I a member of the Round Table."

"I dislike fairy tales," replied the bearded man, the shadow of a smile crossing his lips. "The Grail I seek is real, not folklore. And it is presently lost somewhere in Chicago."

"In Chicago?" repeated Taine, rising from behind the desk. He felt uncomfortable staring at those dark lenses. Ashmedai's face remained a mystery. Taine believed that the eyes reflected a man's soul. Ashmedai kept his hidden for a reason.

The detective looked out the windows of his office onto Lake Michigan. Dark, threatening clouds hovered over the placid waters. Jagged streaks of lightning flared in the late afternoon sky, reflecting the disquiet Taine felt addressing Ashmedai. Clients who spoke in riddles annoyed him.

"You are aware of the theory," said Taine, "that claims the Holy Grail is not the Cup of the Last Supper. That instead, it is the container that held the burial wrappings of Christ, which the same scholars who advocate this position identify as the Shroud of Turin."

Ashmedai shrugged. "I've read *The Shroud and the Grail* by Noel Currer-Briggs. He raises some interesting points. But much of his book is filled with idle speculation. Too often, he manipulates the translations of early legends to fit his hypothesis. Worse, he shows no understanding of the true purpose behind Joseph of Arimathea's actions during and after the Crucifixion."

"Which was?" asked Taine, when Ashmedai hesitated. The stranger spoke with convincing authority about the most mysterious of all occult traditions.

"Currer-Briggs dismissed as utter nonsense the legend that Joseph used the Grail to catch drops of Jesus' blood from the wound made in his side by the Spear of Vengeance. He let his modern sensibilities overcome his scholarly curiosity. Instead of searching for the reason behind Joseph's actions, the author shrugged off the entire episode as tasteless and revolting. Seeking another explanation for the stories linking the Grail and Christ's blood, Currer-Briggs fastened on the blood-stained burial wrappings used by Joseph and Nicodemus. He concluded that the container bearing those blood-marked linens was the true Grail. Extending his theory, he then identified the wrappings as the Shroud of Turin."

Ashmedai chuckled. "A wonderful mental exercise, but absolute nonsense. Joseph of Arimathea knew exactly what he was doing when he caught the Savior's blood in the Grail. For all of his facts, Currer-Briggs refused to acknowledge the reality of the occult."

Taine inhaled sharply, suddenly understanding what Ashmedai meant. "Black magic relies on blood. The blood of Christ…"

"…would work wonders," concluded Ashmedai. "Especially when linked to *Seth's Chalice*."

Taine's eyes narrowed. Few people knew of the existence of that fabled cup. He had learned of it only after years of studying the darkest secrets of the supernatural. Again he wondered, exactly who was Ashmedai? And what were his sources of information?

"According to *The Lost Apocrypha*," said Taine, "when Seth, the third son of Adam and Eve, traveled to the Garden of Eden, he was given a chalice by the Lord as a sign that God had not deserted humanity."

"I'm glad to see your reputation is well deserved. It's hard to believe a mere detective would know of such things."

"I'm not an ordinary detective."

"If you were, I wouldn't be here," replied Ashmedai. "A talisman of incalculable power, the cup passed down through the ages, from generation to generation, held by the greatest mages of the time. Until, finally, it was given as a gift to Jesus by one of his disciples. And became known ever after as the Holy Grail."

"Which you claim is now in Chicago?" said Taine, skepticism creeping into his voice.

"*I know it is.*" The bearded man reached inside his jacket pocket. His hand emerged holding a wad of greenbacks held together by a rubber band. Casually, he dropped the money on Taine's desk.

"I'll pay you five thousand dollars to find the chalice. It belongs to me, and I want it back. No questions asked. If you need more money, let me know."

Taine looked down at the cash, then up at Ashmedai. Down and up again, not saying a word.

"Nothing to worry about, it's honest money. Over the years, I've invested in a number of long-term securities. They pay a handsome return. Money serves me as merely a means to an end."

Still, Taine made no move to pick up the wad. Though he was not above bending the law for his clients when necessary, he held himself to a strict code of ethics, which he refused to compromise. The notion of dealing in stolen religious artifacts crossed that boundary.

"I need a few more details before I'll take this case. You state the Grail belongs to you. What's your claim to it? And how was it stolen?"

"Suspicious, Mr. Taine?" asked Ashmedai, a touch of amusement in his voice. "I assure you, *my right to the chalice is more legitimate than most.*"

The bearded man hesitated, as if considering what to say next. "Details of what happened to the cup after the Crucifixion are shrouded in mystery. Arthurian legend had Joseph traveling to England, taking the Grail with him. Several occult references place the chalice in the hands of Simon the Magician. I've even read an account of it surfacing in the court of Charles the Great, Charlemagne." Ashmedai shook his head, almost in dismay. "No one really knows the truth. Though I suspect it is much less colorful than any of those fables.

"The Grail and Joseph of Arimathea disappeared shortly after Christ's burial. They vanished into the murkiness of ancient history. In time, both became enshrined in legend.

"In 1907, archaeologists at a dig outside of Damascus, Syria, uncovered a spectacular silver chalice with images of the Last Supper engraved in great detail. Comparison to like pieces dated the cup to 5th century A.D.

"After making discreet financial arrangements with certain government officials, the discoverers of the Chalice of

Damascus offered it for sale to the highest bidder. A Syrian antiques dealer, acting as agent for an American millionaire, bought the rarity for $700,000. Like hundreds of other pieces, it disappeared into the reclusive publisher's vast California estate."

"The Chalice of Damascus and the Holy Grail…?"

"Were one and the same. Some enterprising silversmith concealed Seth's Cup beneath a sheath of finely crafted metal. It both protected and concealed the relic. The truth emerged only after an exhaustive scientific testing done at the millionaire's estate. Hidden under a silver lining was the cup of the Last Supper.

"I tried for decades, without success, to purchase the Grail. The new owner refused to let it go. The more I offered, the more obstinate he became. After his death, his estate maintained the same position.

"Finally, this year, facing a huge tax increase and declining revenues due to unwise investments, they relented. It cost me a king's ransom, but the Grail belonged to me."

"Only to be stolen," concluded Taine.

"I never even saw the cup," said Ashmedai bitterly. "Last night, two security guards flew into O'Hare airport with the Grail in their possession. They departed the terminal shortly after nine in the evening, in a hired limo, bound for my estate in northern Illinois. That was the last anyone saw of them."

"The police?"

"They're waiting for a ransom note. The fools are treating the disappearance as an art theft."

"And you don't?"

"The Grail is the most coveted magical talisman in the world. I thought no one other than myself knew its location. Obviously, I believed wrong. Someone stole the chalice and intends to use it for his own ends. What that purpose might be, I have no idea. But knowing the power inherent in the Grail, I shudder at the thought."

There was no mistaking the worry in Ashmedai's voice.

Still, Taine had his doubts about the man. "And your plans for the Grail?"

"If I thought to use the chalice for evil intent, I would've stolen it years ago," said Ashmedai, as if reading Taine's mind. "Instead, I waited, biding my time, and acquired the treasure honestly. My intent has never been criminal. My collection of occult rarities is the greatest in the world. I am assembling it for a purpose that need not concern you. The Grail belongs there, well-guarded and protected, away from the schemes of little men."

Ashmedai's voice grew icy cold. "I am not a man easily crossed, Mr. Taine. Whoever stole the Grail will pay – pay severely."

The detective noted that Ashmedai seemed unconcerned about the fate of the two bodyguards; all the bearded man wanted was the Grail. Nothing else mattered.

"I have a few ideas," said Taine, dropping back into his chair. "Some people to call." He slid a pad of paper and a pen across the desk. "Give me a number where I can reach you."

"Call me day or night," said Ashmedai, scribbling a phone number on the paper. He passed it to Taine.

"Let me know the instant you locate the cup," he said, rising from his chair. "I'll come at once."

"If it can be found, I'll find it."

"That is why I hired you. Good luck."

Somehow, Taine had a feeling he'd need it.

-2-

Seven hours later, the detective wearily pushed open the door to the Spiderweb Lounge on Chicago's northwest side. None of his usual sources had provided a clue to the missing relic. Nor had his own investigations at the airport turned up anything the least bit useful. Much as Taine disliked the notion, the only remaining option was to enter the Spiderweb. And deal with its owner, Sal "The Spider" Albanese.

According to crime insiders, Albanese's nickname came from his involvement in every sort of illegal activity in Chicago. Stolen property, guns, prostitution, drugs, and murder were all part of his everyday business. Like a giant spider, the crime boss spun his deadly web across the Windy City.

Others assumed that the moniker derived from Albanese's appearance. An immensely fat man who favored dark clothing, the elderly gangster bore an uncanny resemblance to a gigantic arachnid. Sal's unwavering gaze and jet-black eyes did nothing to dispel that image.

Only a select group knew of Albanese's youthful encounter with the outer darkness. They had actually seen the incredible scars across the fat man's back and understood the full significance of the title, "The Spider." Sidney Taine, occult investigator, was one such man.

While not an admirer of the gangster, Taine belonged to a certain occult fraternity that included Albanese as well. Which was why he was admitted to the crime chief's office without any hassle.

"Taine," grunted Albanese, waving one huge hand at the detective. In his other, The Spider held a foot-long meatball sandwich. Albanese was always eating, feeding his bloated three-hundred-pound body. "Long time, no see. Join me for a late snack?"

"No thanks," replied Taine. He nodded to Tony Bracco and Leo Scaglia, Albanese's ever-present bodyguards. Tony, short but built like a fireplug, crinkled his eyes in recognition. Leo, tall and thin, who handled a knife with the skill of a surgeon, grinned and nodded. He worked out at the same gym as Taine, and more than once he and the detective had boxed for a few rounds in the sparring ring.

Albanese made short work of the sandwich. Reaching for the tray on his desk, he guzzled down a stein filled with beer, then raised a second meatball hero to his lips.

They chatted for a few minutes, discussing the Bulls, the Bears, and the Cubs. Albanese followed all sports closely.

Making book helped pay the bills. Finally, the gangster got down to business.

"Whatcha here for?" asked Albanese, biting deep into his third sandwich. Carefully, he wiped little drops of meat sauce off his shirt. "From your call I take it this ain't a social visit. You working for the Brotherhood?"

"Not tonight. I'm investigating a robbery. My client is willing to pay quite a bundle for the return of some stolen property. No questions asked. With your contacts, I thought you might be able to help."

"Always glad to help a 'friend.' Whatcha missing?"

"It's a silver cup, a religious artifact known as the Chalice of Damascus."

Sal Albanese froze in mid-bite, his jaws gaping wide open. Seconds passed, and then, very carefully, he put his sandwich down on the desk. "Too messy," he claimed, not very convincingly.

"About the Chalice…?"

"Don't know nothing about no chalice. None of my people have anything to do with robbing relics, Taine. That ain't my style."

Black eyes glared at Taine defiantly, as if challenging the detective to say otherwise. Behind the bluster, Taine sensed something else. Fear. "Are you positive?" Taine tried one more time.

"You doubting my word, Taine?" His huge hands clenched into fists. "I don't like being called a liar."

"No offense, Sal." It made no sense to antagonize the crime boss without good reason. "I just assumed that with all your connections you would have all the details about this theft."

"I ain't heard nothing. Now clear out, Taine. I got business to discuss with the boys. I don't have time for idle chitchat."

Taine turned to leave. Out of the corner of an eye, he caught a furtive gesture by Leo Scaglia. The tall bodyguard, his body half turned so that only Taine could see the signal, moved one hand as if to indicate, "later." The detective dipped his head slightly in acknowledgment, then departed.

-3-

An hour later, back at his office, Taine picked up his phone on the first ring. Scaglia, his voice muffled and barely distinguishable, was on the other end.

"You wanted information on the chalice?" asked the bodyguard, straight off, without any word of greeting. "I know where it is."

"Sal has it?" inquired Taine, not sure what to believe.

"Nah. He won't touch no religious stuff. You know him. But ain't nothing goin' on that Sal don't hear about. He was just too scared to say anything to you at the club. Sal suspects that somebody's passing on all our secrets to those crazy Jamaicans. Bracco's been acting pretty odd lately, flashing a lot of money and making big talk. So the boss had me make this call, private-like. Sal thought you'd want to know the truth. That lunatic, King Wedo, stole your precious chalice."

"King Wedo?" said Taine, taken by surprise. Though he had never met the mysterious Jamaican crime lord, he had heard quite a bit about him. In Chicago for less than a year, the gang leader had earned a reputation as a merciless, violent killer with a taste for the bizarre.

"Sal's frightened and with good reason. Those Jamaican bozos working for King Wedo are crazy. They'd just as soon rip out your guts as look at you. Life is cheap, don't mean a thing to them. Bastards take a dislike to somebody, he's dead meat."

A note of fear crept into Scaglia's voice. "Joey Ventura made the mistake of crossing King Wedo in a business deal. Joey got greedy during a coke delivery and swiped some goods he didn't pay for. Stupid idea. The Jamaicans pulled him right out of a restaurant at lunch time. They shot down three bystanders dumb enough to interfere. Like I said, life don't mean nothin' to them."

Scaglia's voice dropped to a whisper. "King Wedo planned a special finish for Joey. He called it a little demonstration for anyone else with similar ideas. The maniac cut off Joey's fingers and toes, one joint at a time, and forced him to swallow the pieces. It took the poor slob three days to die. Now you understand why Sal's cautious."

"Perfectly. Any clue to why King Wedo clipped the chalice? Ransom perhaps?"

"Nothing definite. But King Wedo don't need the money, not with the dough he's raking in from the drug trade. Word on the street is that the Jamaican is heavy into black magic. Maybe he figures this chalice of yours will give him some sort of mystical powers. Who the hell knows with these crazy bastards."

"Sure," said Taine, his mind racing. King Wedo and the Holy Grail added up to a dangerous mix. He had to retrieve the chalice. "Maybe I should talk to the King about returning the cup. You have any idea where he holds court?"

"You're nuts, man. One wrong word to that geek and he'll carve out your heart. With his fingernails."

"Let me worry about that. Where's his main base?"

"On the near-south side. Around Twenty-sixth and the railroad tracks." The bodyguard hesitated for a moment, then cursed. "The Jamaicans might let you enter their hideout, but they sure the hell won't let you leave. No chance you'll change your mind?"

"Can't. It's my job."

"Well, you'll need some backup. And I guess that means me. I'll meet you there in an hour. Corner of Twenty-sixth and Rand. Don't be late, 'cause if you are, I might just lose my nerve."

"I'll be there," promised Taine and hung up the phone.

-4-

Having changed into his lucky shirt, Taine arrived at the designated location a few minutes after midnight. Amber-colored street lights cast an eerie glow on the otherwise deserted avenue. Huge old warehouses lined both sides of the street, towering into the night sky like ancient tombs.

Soundlessly, Leo beckoned from the doorway of a nearby building. After a quick check of the surroundings, Taine slipped out of his car and joined the mobster.

"What's the story?" whispered Taine.

"We're in luck," replied Scaglia, grinning. "King Wedo and his thugs are out celebrating. One of Sal's contacts spotted them a half-hour ago at the Kozy Klub. We should have no problem finding that chalice and making off with it before the Jamaican returns. Damned SOB is so sure of himself, I doubt he bothered leaving anyone on guard."

"Sounds too easy," said Taine, staring at Scaglia suspiciously. "Why are you so anxious to help, Leo? I never knew you to take unnecessary risks."

"Back off, Taine. Sal's pushing for King Wedo to take a fall. He told me to lend you a hand. Anything that makes King Wedo look bad, makes Sal Albanese look good. I'm following the *capo's* orders. Besides, we're friends."

Leo pushed open the door to the warehouse. "Follow me and don't make a sound. King Wedo's office is in the rear of the building. That's probably where he's keeping the chalice."

The two men crept silently through the huge warehouse. Taine moved with surprising grace for a man his size. Leo Scaglia slithered through the darkness like a giant snake, intent on its prey. Past rows and rows of massive crates filled with unknown goods they slipped, only the soft sound of their breathing breaking the stillness of the stale air. Finally, they reached the rear of the building.

"That's the place," Leo whispered softly in Taine's ear, pointing to the foreman's office located at the junction of two walls. "No lights on. Looks deserted."

Both men pulled out their guns. "You go first," said Scaglia. "You know what to look for. I'll cover you from behind."

Carefully, Taine twisted the knob. It turned effortlessly, not locked. Taking his time, the detective inched open the door. It was as dark inside the office as without. Slowly, ever so slowly, he slipped inside the room.

And found himself staring at a slender black man, sitting behind a wide desk. King Wedo. Waiting with him, standing at his side, were two powerfully built Jamaicans. Both men held Skorpion machine gun pistols aimed at Taine's stomach.

"Mr. Taine," said King Wedo, with a faint smile. "How nice of you to drop by."

Behind Taine, the door swung open. "Sorry, buddy," he heard Leo Scaglia say, "but orders is orders."

Then something hard and unyielding crashed down on his skull and he heard nothing else.

-5-

When Taine regained consciousness, he found himself securely bound to a heavy wood chair. He was in the same room, now brightly illuminated. King Wedo faced him on the other side of a wide desk. The two massive bodyguards, guns nowhere to be seen, stood behind their boss's chair. Leo, arms folded across his chest, lolled against a metal filing cabinet.

"*You're* the informer in Albanese's organization," said Taine, disgusted by his own stupidity, "not Bracco."

"So what else is new? When I called the King and told him you were fishing for the chalice, he ordered me to reel you in. Easiest assignment I ever had. You didn't suspect nothin'."

"I'm too naïve for my own good," said Taine. Whoever had tied him to the chair had taken his gun, as well as the knife sheathed to his ankle. Luckily, they had missed the razor blades concealed in his shirt cuffs. Cautiously, he started sawing at the ropes binding his wrists. "For some reason, I still trust my fellow man."

"A bad habit, Mr. Taine," said King Wedo, with a shake of his head. The Jamaican spoke softly but distinctly, with the barest trace of an English accent. "Especially for a private investigator. But of course, you are no ordinary detective. Which is why I instructed Leo to bring you here instead of ordering your execution. You are going to prove very useful to me, Mr. Taine. Very, very useful."

Reaching into a drawer of the desk, King Wedo pulled out a plain wooden goblet. Though the chalice's origin dated back thousands of years, there was not a scratch on it.

"The Holy Grail. Stripped of that foolish silver decoration, it appears to be incredibly ordinary. But as we all well know, looks can be deceiving." King Wedo rose from his chair, balancing the cup in one hand. A slender man with pleasant features, only his narrow, mad eyes betrayed the cruelty lurking within. He circled the desk so that he stood only a few feet from Taine.

"Consider me, for example. I am notorious as a crazy gangster. An image I work hard to cultivate. Fear serves me well, Mr. Taine. Still, none of my enemies or my friends suspect that I am also a master of black magic. Only a select few even realize that sorcery exists.

"In my youth, I attended school in England. My father, a wealthy plantation owner, had dreams of me expanding the family business. Even then, I had *other plans*.

"You can imagine my surprise when I discovered, quite by accident, that my history professor was a practicing black magician. I discovered him placing a curse on one of his faculty rivals. Sensing my interest in the dark art, he made me his apprentice." The Jamaican's eyes narrowed. "For a price, of course."

Taine grimaced. Sorcerers always demanded payment for their services. A fee paid in blood.

"The professor and I parted on good terms nearly a decade ago. Never once during the intervening years did I hear from him."

Taine remained silent, busily sawing away at the ropes

with his razor blade. Gangsters loved to brag about their accomplishments. Like most psychopaths, King Wedo was consumed by a desire to display his brilliance. Surrounded by thugs and assorted lowlifes, the Jamaican reveled in the chance to show off for Taine. Which meant the gangster planned to murder him afterwards. Dead men never betrayed secrets.

"Then a week ago, I suddenly received a call from him. The old man told me the Holy Grail was being shipped to Chicago. The professor requested my aid in stealing the relic and promised me fabulous riches for my cooperation. I agreed to help. But my arrangements benefited only me.

"My men intercepted the Grail messengers, killed them both, and made off with the chalice. Instead of turning it over to the professor, I kept the cup for myself. The old fool should have known better than to trust someone like me. I have plans for the Grail. Plans that concern you, Mr. Taine."

A cold chill swept through Taine. "Why me?" he asked. Anything to stall for a little more time. Cutting through the ropes was proving more difficult than he anticipated. "What makes me special?"

"I know all about you, Mr. Taine. Those who practice the black arts like to keep close tabs on their adversaries. And I believe that description fits you very well. *Adversary.*" Gently, King Wedo placed Seth's Cup on his desk. Crossing his arms across his chest, he shook his head in mock dismay. "If I am an evil soul, my friend, then by definition, are you not a good one? A righteous one?"

Taine shuddered. King Wedo's words struck a chord deep within his being. He finally understood what the Jamaican had planned – an ancient rite of dark magic, of blood sorcery. Evidently the concern showed in his face. The gang leader chuckled.

"Seven drops of blood from a righteous soul," he recited, using words of frightening power, "if the Cup of Purity is thy goal."

King Wedo strolled back around the desk and dropped

back in his chair. He reached into a desk drawer and pulled out a plastic bag filled with white powder. "Coke. Good stuff, but not perfect. *Not pure.*" The Jamaican leaned forward, his gaze fastened on his prisoner. "The purer the dope, the better the hit. That's the story on cocaine. Even the dumbest crackhead knows it. Problem is that no system filters out all the impurities in the drug. No matter how fine you make it, the stuff ain't perfect. It's never totally pure."

"You don't intend..." began Taine, shocked by the Jamaican's plan.

"Ah, but I do. I do. According to all of the medieval legends, *the Holy Grail purifies whatever it touches.* The mere contact with the cup changes water into wine, poor man's bread into cake. Well, we're going to see if those stories are true." The Jamaican opened the bag holding the cocaine. "Think of the rush, Mr. Taine. Imagine the purest cocaine in the world – available only from me. I'll be able to name my price."

King Wedo beckoned Scaglia closer. "You got your knife handy, Leo?"

Scaglia pulled out a six-inch switchblade. With a bare whisper of sound, the metal blade glittered in the harsh light. "Never go anywhere without it."

"Take the cup and christen it with seven drops of Mr. Taine's blood."

"Whatever you say," said Scaglia, delicately balancing the switchblade in one hand, the wooden cup in the other. "You want me to cut his throat?"

"Leo, Leo, Leo," said King Wedo, sounding properly shocked. "How wasteful. The formula calls for the blood of a righteous man each time we perform the ceremony. We don't have an endless supply of righteous men in Chicago." The gang leader's voice turned grim. "We must make Mr. Taine last a long, *long* time."

"You're the boss," said Scaglia, shrugging his shoulders. He slipped the cold steel beneath a button of Taine's lucky shirt. With a flick of the wrist, the hood slashed through the thin material up to the detective's neck.

"Tough break, buddy," he muttered, bending close with the Cup of Seth. "But orders is orders."

Another slash of the knife. A thin red ribbon blossomed across Taine's chest. Carefully, Scaglia collected his bounty.

"Seven drops," warned King Wedo. "No more, no less."

The gang leader opened the plastic bag holding the cocaine. Using his pinky, he stirred the white powder. "From what I've read, the blood activates the magical properties of the cup instantly. Let's see what it does with the coke."

Scaglia growled – a beast-like sound rising from deep within his chest. A mad noise that caught all of them by surprise. Taine's eyes blinked in shock as the Grail-bearer's features twisted with sudden fury.

"You dirty son of a bitch!" Scaglia shouted and grabbed for his gun. But Wedo's men were faster.

Weapons exploded, and the room filled with the sound and smell of gunfire. Scaglia's body erupted in blood. Like a grotesque, drunken marionette, he staggered back and forth, driven by the fury of the bullets slamming into his torso.

"Be careful of the cup!" shrieked King Wedo, standing, only his voice betraying any sign of panic. "Don't hit it."

Hot blood gushing from a dozen wounds, Scaglia should have been dead but wasn't. Only his burning will kept him alive. He pulled his gun free and returned fire.

Taine, not sure he understood what was taking place, wrenched hard on the last few strands of cord imprisoning his hands. The rope snapped, and the detective dropped to the floor. Unarmed, he was not crazy enough to attack either Scaglia or Wedo's cronies.

The shooting stopped as abruptly as it began. Silence echoed through the small office. Both bodyguards were down – one shot through the heart, the second man's nose a red ruin where a bullet had crashed up and through to his brain. Scaglia lay sprawled across King Wedo's desk, the Grail clutched tightly in one hand. Amazingly, a spark of life still flickered in his eyes.

"I don't like traitors, Leo," said King Wedo, rising up from the floor on the other side of his desk, a stiletto tightly gripped in one hand. He spoke calmly, without the least trace of malice. "You took my money to betray your boss. But evidently, he paid you even more to double-cross me." King Wedo shook his head. "Bad choice, Leo."

"You scum," Scaglia managed to gasp out, his mad eyes burning with hatred. "No one paid..."

"Enough lies," said King Wedo. With a savage twist of the knife, he ripped the blade across Leo's throat. Leo's body arched in agony as his life blood poured out onto the wood desk. One last gasp, and he was dead.

"Don't try anything, Mr. Taine." A .45 automatic appeared in King Wedo's hand as if by magic. He never even glanced at the dead man. "Please rise very slowly from the floor. And keep both of your hands in plain sight."

Taine stood up. At this range, King Wedo couldn't miss. The Jamaican seemed unruffled by the violence that had taken place during the past few minutes.

"I never panic," said King Wedo, as if reading the detective's mind. Careful never to shift his eyes away from Taine, the gang leader reached for the Holy Grail. "That's why I always come out on top. That's why I'm the king."

Wrapping his fingers around the edge of the wooden goblet, King Wedo pulled the Grail free of Scaglia's grip. "I thought I could trust Leo, but I guess not. No matter."

The muzzle of the automatic never wavered. "Two can keep a secret if one of them is dead, Mr. Taine," said King Wedo. "Goodbye."

Desperately, the detective flung himself to the side. One of the dead bodyguards still held a gun. It was a forlorn hope, but Taine's only chance. He scrambled for the weapon, expecting any second to hear the roar of King Wedo's automatic and feel the impact of a slug in his back.

Taine whirled, the dead man's weapon in hand. Then came to a sudden stop, caught completely by surprise.

King Wedo stood frozen in place. Sweat glistened on his

forehead. Madness twisted his face in a grimace of incredible pain. The .45 automatic no longer threatened Taine. Instead, its muzzle touched against the gangster's forehead. Wild eyes met Taine's in a silent plea for help. But there was no time left. King Wedo's finger jerked hard against the trigger. The gun roared once, then fell silent.

-6-

"An interesting if not surprising tale," said the man called Ashmedai. "Many legends refer to the Grail as the Cup of Treachery. A title it has well earned. Too many men have been betrayed by it. I wonder if this King Wedo ever grasped the truth?"

"I think he did," said Taine, staring at the Holy Grail resting on the desk top between them. "In that last instant, I believe he realized the trap into which he had fallen. But by then, holding the cup, there was nothing he could do. In a way, it was a grim sort of justice for his crimes."

Ashmedai shrugged and reached for the chalice. "The fools never understand that the Grail turns all that come in contact with it pure. Including those men foolish enough to hold it."

"The conflict in their souls destroyed them both. Repentance was not enough. Scaglia could no longer serve evil, so he tried to destroy it. And King Wedo, overwhelmed by his monstrous crimes, resorted to suicide." He paused. "Do you dare risk taking it? I carried it here in a box I discovered in King Wedo's office. I never touched it myself."

"I am unaffected by the spell," said Ashmedai confidently, lifting the Grail. "Joseph was no fool when he covered the cup in silver. No ordinary mortal could touch the chalice and live with himself afterwards. No man is that pure."

The bearded man examined the cup carefully, a wistful smile playing across his lips. "So many years – so many years."

"Now that you have it..."

"The Grail goes into my collection, where it will remain out of the sight of man until it's needed."

"You called it the Cup of Treachery?" asked Taine, puzzled. In all of his studies of the occult, he had never encountered the phrase before.

Ashmedai lowered the chalice to the desk. Two-thousand-year-old eyes stared at Taine from behind dark lenses. His voice sounded weary, terribly so. "The chalice was a gift to Christ from one of his disciples. One who doubted and thought to use the Grail as a final test. And thus began a tale of treachery – and eternal damnation."

Ashmedai sighed. "Now do you understand?"

"Yes," answered Taine, no longer curious to see the eyes behind those glasses.

TERROR BY NIGHT

"Four people gone without a trace," said the bald-headed man, his voice trembling. Nervously, he rubbed the back of an arm across his forehead, wiping at oily beads of sweat with a stained white shirt sleeve. "All of them vanished, as if into thin air. Not a sign of a scuffle or anything suspicious. One a week, for the past month. Another office worker turns up missing. They work late into the night. The next morning, they're gone. It's spooked the whole building. Nobody stays after hours anymore. Several tenants have moved out. And more are threatening to break their leases."

The two men sat across a desk in a windowless office on the ground floor of a mid-sized office building. The building was nestled in the heart of the Chicago Loop and gave no outward appearance of the evil that hid inside its walls. The Styrofoam cups of coffee that sat before them had long since gone cold.

"You're positive the victims all disappeared while on the premises?" asked Sidney Taine. A big, powerfully-built man, he spoke in calm, even-measured tones. His dark eyes stared intently at the building superintendent.

"Unfortunately, yes," said Sam Shaw, his upper teeth gnawing on his lower lip. "There's always a security guard at the desk in the front hall. No one can enter or leave the building without passing him. Joe Frost is a retired cop who works the night shift. He swears that none of the four left the complex."

"What do the police say?"

"They say Joe must be mistaken." Shaw sounded disgusted. "For all their investigating and hunting for clues, the cops are as much in the dark as the rest of us. That's why I turned to you."

Taine nodded. He specialized in cases involving supernatural or supernormal manifestations. One newspaper had gone so far as to dub him "The New Age Detective."

Nicknames mattered little to Taine. His main concern was solving crimes. A skilled investigator as well as an expert in the occult sciences, he used whatever methods necessary to discover the truth.

"I'll need an office and a cover story to quell any suspicions."

"You think someone working in the building is behind the disappearances?" asked Shaw. His voice caught in his throat. "That's hard to believe. I've known some of these people for twenty years."

"Let's not jump to any conclusions. For all we know, the police could be right. Maybe Frost is getting forgetful and doesn't want to admit it."

"No," said Shaw, with a shake of his head. "That isn't true. I know it and I suspect so do you. There's something unnatural preying on the tenants here. I can feel its presence, feel it in my bones. Something…evil."

Taine nodded. "After twenty years of managing these offices, your inner eye, your 'sixth sense,' has become attuned to the physical structure of the building itself. On a subconscious level, your spirit suffers with each crime committed on the grounds. You are as much a part of this place as the stones in its foundation."

The big detective rose smoothly from his chair. "Time for me to earn my pay. I'll want to meet Joe Frost before we go up to my new office. And anyone else who works the night shift."

"That would be the cleaning woman, Roska Smith. She sweeps the offices after everyone leaves. She's a refugee from

Iran or Iraq or someplace like that. Her real name is absolutely unpronounceable, so I call her Mrs. Smith."

"I assume the police checked out her background thoroughly?"

"Of course. She's worked here for more than a year without any problems. Mr. Larson, the owner of the building, called me from Florida and told me to hire her. Evidently, he met her overseas and promised her a job if she ever emigrated to the United States. A quiet, dependable, and very hardworking woman. I've never had a complaint about her from any of the tenants."

Shaw pushed open the door to his office. "There's an empty suite on the fifth floor. I'll set you up there."

Taine followed the superintendent down a narrow service corridor to the front of the building. They emerged in a wide foyer where a lone guard sat reading a newspaper that rested on an ancient wood desk. Behind him creaked and groaned a pair of equally aged elevators.

A short, stocky man with wide shoulders and a barrel chest, Frost's hair matched his name. Cut short, it was as white as snow. He nodded a greeting to Shaw as the two men approached. The guard eyed Taine with undisguised curiosity. Closing the newspaper, he stood up as they came nearer.

"Joe Frost, meet Sidney Paine," said Shaw, using the name they had agreed upon during their phone conversation. There was no need to alert anyone else about a private investigator in the building. "Mr. Paine is leasing the Burnham office on the fifth floor. He'll move in tomorrow. I'm showing him around the building tonight."

The two men shook hands. Though Taine estimated Frost to be in his early sixties, the retired cop had the powerful grip of a man half his age. With a grin, the security guard squeezed hard, testing Taine's strength. Taine ignored the pressure. His massive hand remained firm and unyielding. Finally Frost nodded and let go.

"Your hand ain't soft like some pencil pusher," said the guard. He squinted, as if trying to remember something forgotten. "Seems to me I read about a man with a name like yours in the paper awhile back. According to the reporter, this guy was a detective specializing in unusual cases. Kind of implied he was some sort of occult Sherlock Holmes. Big man too, around six-one, six-two – two-twenty, or so. Right around your size, Mr. *Paine*."

"Two-ten," replied Taine, with the hint of a smile. The old police veteran was no fool. "I've been on a diet. What's your theory about these disappearances, Frost? I can't imagine much going on in this building without your knowing about it."

Worry lines not in evidence a minute before suddenly lined his face, and his voice sunk down to a whisper. "Crooks I know how to deal with. But these is ghosts." He continued in a voice that was flat and yet, somehow, filled with apprehension. "In the middle of the night, I hear their voices in the walls. They don't speak in words, just sounds – weird, garbled, *chittering* noises. Mr. Shaw claims it's water dripping in the heating system down in the basement. But that ain't what I'm hearing. The damned building is haunted."

"Nonsense. You're imagining things, Frost." Shaw didn't sound very convincing.

The security guard started to reply, then froze. He cocked his head to one side, listening. "Am I?" he asked, his mouth twisted in a crooked grin. "Maybe you want to explain…that?"

There was no mistaking exactly to what Frost referred. The hallway reverberated with a soft, wind-like whisper that seemed to come from everywhere and nowhere. Shaw sucked in a breath, his face bleached white. Taine stepped to the near wall and placed one ear against the ancient plasterboard. Faintly, ever so distantly, he could hear the echo of unintelligible voices. In a second, they were gone.

"The rats," muttered Taine, more to himself than the others. "The rats in the walls."

"There are no vermin in my building," declared Shaw, his voice shrill with fear.

Taine shook his head. Shaw was not the type to read H.P. Lovecraft. "Let's see that office now."

Frost waved almost cheerfully as they stepped into one of the elevators. Taine suspected the guard was relieved that they had heard the whispering voices. The old cop had probably wondered many times if the noises were real or the product of an aging mind. Now he knew that he was sane. Or that they were all mad.

Hissing and wheezing, the lift deposited them on the fifth floor. Dim lights sent flickering shadows scurrying across the walls as the two men marched down the hallway. Odd, barely-visible patterns crawled across the threadbare carpeting beneath their feet. Even the stale air in the corridor seemed heavy with age.

Surprisingly, the interior of suite 511 was quite modern. A sleek, laminated desk complete with a wheeled, well-cushioned chair and newly-tiled floor dominated the room. Behind it, sitting neatly on a table in the corner, was a brand new copier and fax machine. Not a scratch marred the black metal file cabinets on the far wall.

"Burnham ran an insurance scam from the office," said Shaw, answering the unasked question. "He came in once or twice a week to meet with the suckers. The rest of the time the place stayed empty. The FBI finally nailed him last month for mail fraud, but they were too late. Burnham skipped town the day before they came looking for him."

Taine filed the story away for future consideration. Another disappearance from the same building, whatever the explanation, stretched coincidence beyond probability.

"Here's the key. The phone and fax machine are disconnected, but other than that, the office is exactly the way Burnham left it.

"How long do you think this will take? I'm paying your fee out of my own salary. Larson couldn't care less what happens here. He inherited the property from his father. For the past fifteen years, he's lived in Florida and conducted his business by phone. All he cares about is his check every month.

If a few more tenants break their leases, he'll probably close the place down and sell the land for a shopping mall. Leaving me," Shaw concluded bitterly, "with nothing."

"What about the cleaning lady, Mrs. Smith?"

"I almost forgot about her. She works one floor at a time, starting up at the top with number seven. That puts her on this floor around midnight. Don't expect too much from Mrs. Smith. She doesn't speak English very well and keeps pretty much to herself. Like most refugees, she's not anxious to make waves."

"I won't upset her. Though I am hoping she knows what those noises were we heard downstairs."

"The pipes," said Shaw, without conviction. "It was just the pipes." He tried to smother a gaping, tooth-filled yawn. "I'm sorry, Mr. Taine. I haven't had a good night's sleep since this mess began."

"Go home and get some sleep," Taine said. "The building is in good hands. I'll let you know if something turns up."

The superintendent departed, leaving Taine alone in the office. Suppressing a yawn of his own, the big detective stretched his arms high over his head. Another case had kept him up late the past few evenings. He had been looking forward to a good night's sleep tonight.

Reaching into his jacket pocket, Taine pulled out a thick sheaf of papers. After Shaw's original phone call, the detective had called in a few favors. After sending a few faxes to some knowledgeable friends, he had stopped at the local police station and picked up copies of the police reports filed on the four disappearances. He doubted there would be much in the files, but Taine took no chances on missing anything.

He spent the next two hours poring over the papers. As he suspected, there was nothing very surprising in any of them. In fact, the most telling bit of information Taine gleaned from the reports was the dissimilarity of the missing people.

Two men and two women, they came from different age

groups and different income levels. One was in middle management; two were office workers; and the fourth was the sole proprietor of a talent agency. Three out of the four were over forty, while the last had just turned twenty-two. Two were Black; one was Caucasian; and one Hispanic. None of them had any links to professional crime figures or gamblers. The one word that best described all four was "ordinary."

Taine sighed and leaned back in his chair. Like the police, he could find no motive for the disappearances. No facts tied the quartet together. They were as mismatched a group to be found. The only thing they had in common was the building.

A soft knock at his office door interrupted his train of thought. "Come in."

A tall woman, clad in a brown shirt and overalls, pushed open the door. Her weather-beaten face was dark brown, almost the color and texture of old leather. She had pitch-black hair, tied up tightly in a bun, and matching deep black eyes.

"Sorry, sorry," she said, her voice thick with a singsong Arabic accent. "I did not mean to disturb." Behind her Taine glimpsed a big-wheeled bin lined with an immense brown canvas sack for garbage, with a half-dozen brooms and dusters stuck in the sides. "I will be pleased to come back later."

"No problem," said Taine, getting out of his chair. "I wasn't doing anything important. Please," he beckoned with one hand, "come in."

"I will only be a minute," said Mrs. Smith, wheeling in the bin. She pulled out a wide-based broom and dust pan. Without another word, she quickly started sweeping the office floor, cleaning to Taine's left.

Taine moved out of her way and watched her work. The woman moved silently, with a smooth, sensuous grace that he founded vaguely unsettling. From time to time, she glanced up at him and smiled, a close-lipped smile.

"This seems like a nice building," said Taine casually. "A little old, but otherwise well maintained."

"Very nice," said Mrs. Smith, her head nodding in agreement as she swept. Finishing up, she emptied the dust pan into the brown garbage sack. Replacing her broom, she checked the garbage can at the base of the desk for clutter.

"Funny how the pipes make such strange noises though," continued Taine. "They almost sound like human voices crying in agony."

Mrs. Smith's black eyes widened. "Voices? No, no. It is sound of pipes, nothing more. Mr. Shaw tell me himself. It is pipes."

The cleaning woman was afraid, very afraid. Taine wondered what could frighten her so badly. He took for granted that she would never tell a stranger the reason.

Without another word, Mrs. Smith pushed her bin back into the hall and pulled the office door closed after her. Taine could hear her hurriedly wheeling the cart down the hallway in the direction of the elevators. In a minute, she was gone, the other offices on the floor untouched.

The detective frowned. The woman's unusual behavior left him more puzzled than ever. He felt sure she knew something about the strange noises. She appeared terrified by their very mention. Yet she echoed Shaw's outlandish remark about the pipes.

Behind him, the fax machine beeped. Taine turned and stared at the unit. A quick glance at the outlet confirmed Shaw's earlier statement. The machine wasn't plugged in. And yet it was working.

As Taine watched, a solitary sheet of paper worked its way through the processor and into the document tray. Then, with a click audible throughout the small room, the machine that could not possibly be functioning shut itself off.

Taine picked up the document. Not surprisingly, the sender's name was not listed at the top of the page. However, the detective felt sure he knew the source of the transmission. For years, there had been rumors, odd tales, of a secret society fighting supernatural horror throughout the world. Taine knew the rumors were true. They called themselves the

Societas Argenti Viae Eternitata, the Eternal Society of the Silver Way. He was positive that this message came from that mysterious group, returning his favor.

Curious, he looked at the paper. The only marking on it was a number at the direct center of the page. The number 91.

Taine's brows knitted in concentration. It took tremendous occult power to send a message by supernatural means, the shortness of the transmission not withstanding. Yet the mages of S.A.V.E. evidently believed that the solitary number provided enough of a warning for Taine. It was on his shoulders to decipher the clue.

The product of two mystic primes, 7 and 13, 91 was a great power. Many powerful spells consisted of ninety-one syllables, ninety-one words, or ninety-one sentences. Taine closed his eyes in concentration. The thought of spells and warnings had his subconscious bubbling. Buried deep in his memory was a vague recollection of a famous quote associated with the number 91. After a few seconds, he understood the reference. And grasped the implied threat.

"Thou shalt not be afraid for the terror by night," recited Taine aloud, *"nor for the arrow that flieth by day; nor the pestilence that walketh in darkness; nor for the destruction that wasteth at noonday."* The warning was a line from the 91st Psalm, long regarded as a powerful warding spell against demons.

Taine reached into his shoulder holster and pulled out his .45 automatic. Positive he knew the truth, he felt safer with the gun in hand. Carefully, he pushed open the door to the office. No one was about.

Using his lock-pick, he broke into three nearby offices before he found what he wanted. In a suite, someone had set up a lunch center, complete with a mini-refrigerator and microwave oven. A few seconds of searching turned up a half-filled salt shaker. Satisfied with his discovery, Taine dropped it into his coat pocket and headed for the elevator.

The sound of snoring greeted him as the lift came to a stop on the first floor. Head on his desk, Joe Frost was solidly submerged in slumber. He didn't stir when Taine walked past, heading for the heavy metal fire door that led to the basement.

It was thirteen steps down to the cellar. A few scattered forty-watt light bulbs provided the only illumination. Eyes narrowed in the gloom, Taine made his way through a maze of old boxes, maintenance equipment, and rusting file cabinets. Filling the center of the room was a massive old furnace, pipes leading from it to a half-dozen upward ducts.

The faint sound of a human voice was all but hidden by the constant rumbling of the boiler. Gun in hand, Taine made his way around the furnace.

A dozen feet away a large trapdoor opened to a black hole in the floor. Mrs. Smith, her back to Taine, knelt there on her knees, jabbering away in a language he didn't recognize. Every few seconds she paused and took a bite from what looked like a turkey drumstick she held tightly in her right hand.

Gingerly, Taine edged his way closer, trying not to make a sound. He kept his automatic pointed directly at the woman's back. At the same time, he worked frantically with his other hand, trying to remove the top of the salt shaker he had taken.

Without warning, Mrs. Smith spun around. Taine gasped in shock. The woman's face was smeared with blood. Confirming his worst fears, he saw that the object she gnawed upon was a human arm. Flesh and muscle had been stripped away right down to the bone. Bright red droplets fell from Mrs. Smith's chin as her lips stretched back into a snarl that revealed a mouthful of hyena-like incisors.

Shaken to his soul, Taine involuntarily took a step backward. That was all the time the woman needed. Howling, she flung the half-devoured limb like a spear, straight at the detective's chest. Reflexively, Taine raised his arms to block the blow.

Mrs. Smith leapt at him. Covering the space between them in an instant, she slammed headfirst into Taine, sending him sprawling to the ground. His automatic went flying into the darkness. Clawing like some wild beast, Mrs. Smith straddled him. Flat on his back, the detective fought for his life against a nightmarish creature intent on his death.

Mrs. Smith's teeth gnashed together inches from his throat. His forearm, wedged up against the woman's neck, was the only thing holding her back. She hissed like some giant serpent as they fought. Taine could feel her hot breath like the fires of hell burning across his eyes.

Mrs. Smith's long fingers dug hard into Taine's shoulders, trying to raise him off the ground. He struggled to stay down. A little closer and she could rip his features to ribbons. Taine was a powerful man, but the woman's strength was incredible. Only the awkwardness of her position enabled him to hold her off. Little by little, she was forcing his arm back and her jaws nearer to his face.

Desperately, Taine shoved his other hand into his coat pocket. Miraculously, the salt shaker was still there. With a final twist of his fingers, he had the cap off.

Sensing something was wrong, Mrs. Smith tightened her legs around his chest. But Taine already had his arm free and moving. The hand clutching the shaker swung up in a half-circle aimed directly at the monster's face. A stream of ordinary kitchen salt caught her right below the eyes.

Mrs. Smith screamed in agony. It was as if Taine had thrown a beaker of acid. The detective could hear her skin sizzling like bacon frying on a griddle. Shrieking in pain, the woman tumbled off Taine and rolled onto the floor, both her hands clutched to her burning face.

Taine scrambled to his feet, his gaze wildly sweeping the room, looking for his gun. The salt wouldn't stop Mrs. Smith for long. He spotted the weapon a dozen feet away, at the base of the furnace. Taine flung himself forward, hands groping for the pistol.

Behind him, Mrs. Smith shrieked again, this time in anger not agony. The detective spun around, one hand clutching his gun, to see the woman charging at him. There was no time to think. Without taking time to aim, Taine squeezed the trigger. And kept on squeezing until the magazine was empty.

The bullets smashed into Mrs. Smith like blows from a giant hammer. Wordlessly, she collapsed to the ground, all the life gone out of her. Far below the floor, the mindless chittering started again.

"What the hell happened here?" demanded Joe Frost, emerging from behind the furnace, his gun drawn. "I heard the commotion upstairs and came down to investigate."

The security guard gasped when he saw the dead body on the floor. "Mrs. Smith?"

"Take a look at her before you make any snap judgments," said Taine, wearily. He holstered his gun. "She's the one behind the disappearances."

Frost bent down to examine the corpse. He cursed in horror. Most of the skin on Mrs. Smith's face was eaten away. Flashes of white bone glistened in the dim light. Revealed as well were the animal fangs that lined her jaw.

"What did this to her?" asked Frost, his voice shaky.

"Common, ordinary, table salt," said Taine. He walked over to the trap door and peered down into the darkness. "I take it this leads down into the sub-basement."

"Yeah, but nobody's been down there for years."

From below came the infernal sound of high-pitched chittering. Frost sucked in a breath, turning white. "That's the sound I heard upstairs."

"Carried through the pipes," said Taine. Reaching down, he grabbed at Mrs. Smith's blouse and ripped. The cloth tore free from her body, revealing her naked flesh beneath.

"Mother-of-God," Frost swore, staring at the woman's nude body. Even Taine, knowing what to expect, was shocked to silence.

Beneath her clothes, Mrs. Smith wasn't even faintly human. Her body had the free flowing form of a wolf or hyena, complete with two rows of nipples that stretched from her upper chest to her lower abdomen. Dark fur covered her flesh like a cloak.

"What – what – is she?" Frost managed to ask.

"A *ghul*," replied Taine. "A creature described in ancient Middle East legends. In The Bible, they are obliquely referred to as 'the terror by night.'" Taine saw no reason to mention the mystic warning he received that alerted him to the presence of such a monster in the building.

"*Ghuls* closely resemble humans. Over the centuries, they've learned to imitate our ways quite well. Which is necessary for them since we provide them with their food. Their diet consists primarily of the *flesh and blood of the people they kill*. Eaters of the dead, they are creatures of pestilence and decay. That is why salt, a preserving agent, burns their flesh."

"You mean…" stuttered Frost, "the people that disappeared…"

Taine pointed at the half-eaten arm. "The rest of the corpse she threw down there." He pointed to the sub-basement.

"Down there?" repeated Frost.

"Once I realized that Mrs. Smith was a *ghul*," said Taine, "I quickly understood the one thing all of her victims had in common. *They were human.* Nothing more than that. She was murdering them for food.

"Without any apparent motive, no one ever suspected her of the killings. I suspect chance played a large part in selecting her victims. Whenever she found herself alone in an office with an unsuspecting worker, she struck. With teeth like those, she could kill in an instant. Her canvas bag could easily hold a body, especially after she ripped it to pieces."

Frost turned green and looked ready to pass out. "But why now? She's worked here for over a year."

Taine pointed down into the sub-basement. Both he and Frost peered into the darkness. A half-dozen pair of glowing red eyes stared back up at them. Odd, twisted shapes, only faintly human, clustered around a half-devoured corpse.

Then, with a wild, high-pitched chittering, the creatures disappeared into the total blackness outside the square of light.

"That's why," said Taine. "Until now, she suckled her young. Lately, though, they required meat – raw meat. That was why she started killing – to provide food for her children."

Frost shook his head in dismay. "What are we going to do with them?"

Taine slammed the trap door shut and bolted it closed. "Leave them for now." Taine wasn't an expert at *ghul* eradication, but he suspected his mysterious friends at S.A.V.E. would know the number for a very special kind of exterminator. "Shaw can send me my check."

The detective stood silent for a second. "When you explain things to your boss tomorrow, pass along this warning. Mr. Larson, the owner, may have something more insidious planned for this building than just a shopping mall. *Ghuls* aren't that much different than human beings. Sexually, the two races are quite compatible. *Someone had to father those monsters in the sub-basement.* If I remember correctly, it was Larsen who insisted that Mrs. Smith be hired."

"Son of a bitch," muttered Frost.

"Not exactly," replied Taine, "but close enough."

...Sid and Sydney Taine are brother and sister. Sort of. They live eight hundred miles and eighteen dimensions apart. Sid is the serious one while Sydney is more the trickster. Sidney investigates the occult. Sydney is part of it.

ENTER, THE ERADICATOR!

Night covered Empire City like a shroud. Thick clouds blocked the moon and stars, and the only illumination came from thousands of city street lamps. At 79th Street and Central Park West, the overhead lights were out, transforming a normally dark area into a black pit. A handful of yellow night-lights glowing in the windows of the Rose Center for Earth and Space, the huge stone and brick research centre, museum, and observatory, provided the only illumination in the neighborhood.

Across the street from the Rose Center, in the shadow of the tall trees of Central Park, stood a solitary figure dressed in a heavy overcoat with an upturned collar and a floppy black slouch hat. The man's features were completely hidden. Only his long slender fingers were visible, holding a copy of the evening edition of the *Empire Times*. If anyone had been standing nearby, they would have immediately noticed that the man was wearing bright red gloves. But at midnight on a cold, cold night in February, no one was foolish enough to be out and around in Central Park. At least, no one sane.

Chuckling softly to himself, the man looked down at his newspaper. It was open to page fifteen. The lead banner proclaimed, *Rose Center Opens New Display*. Beneath the words was a photo of a huge red ruby resting in a glass case, and a paragraph of explanation:

> Huge collection of rare gems found in meteors are stars of the show. Highlight of the exhibit is the incredible Red Ruby of Mercury, the largest ruby in existence. This magnificent jewel was discovered in the heart of the giant Lost Lake meteor 74 years ago. The unique gem is owned by the American Astronomy Society, and this is the first time it's ever been on display.

"First and last," whispered the man, crumpling up the newspaper and dropping it to the street. Sometimes, he talked to himself, spoke to the voices that chattered inside his skull. Explained his plans to them, seeking their approval. Informed the Gods of Chaos and Pandemonium how he was serving them. They liked being kept up to date. "First and last," he said slightly louder as he crossed the street, heading for the Rose Center's front gate.

Two massive ironwood and steel doors, ten feet high and four feet wide, set in the center of a reinforced red brick and concrete wall guarded the building entrance. *Visiting Hours – Noon till 5:00 P.M. Monday through Saturday*, read the press-on letters in the middle of a glass and aluminium sign standing a few feet in front of the doors.

"How inhospitable," muttered the man with the red gloves. Gently he tapped on the doors' steel frame three times. "Knock, knock. Anybody home?"

The building remained quiet. High above the entranceway, two video cameras recorded everything that transpired in their range. Images were scanned, analysed, and rated by high-speed computers every thirty seconds. Even the smallest threats, ranging from an inquisitive squirrel to a gang of thieves, were reported to the Central Park Police Station. The machines were perfect guardians: they couldn't be bribed, never grew tired or bored, and remained totally devoid of emotions. They served and protected. Yet when the man with the red gloves reached inside his coat and pulled out what looked like a golden flute, they didn't sound an alarm. When he raised the flute to his lips and played a series of six notes, they remained quiet. Even when the steel and iron-wood doors seemed to shiver, ripple, and ultimately collapse into a stack of metal shavings and sawdust, the computers stayed silent. Hours later, when the videotapes were finally replayed, they were found to be absolutely blank. Serving the Gods of Chaos and Pandemonium had some privileges.

Casually, the man with the flute stepped over the wreckage of the door and entered the great hall of the Rose Center. He glanced around, like a tourist searching for a special attraction. Finally, he spotted a sign with an arrow pointing upward. *Red Ruby of Mercury, 2nd Floor.* Scanning the huge promenade, the man located a wide span of marble steps leading upward to his prize. He took one step forward, then stopped short.

"Halt!" There was a guard, with a gun, to his left.

"Don't move!" cried a second guard, also armed, from his right.

"Hold it right there!" sang the third, from the top of the marble staircase.

The man in the heavy coat raised his hands straight up over his head. In doing so, he released the pair of metal clamps that held his overcoat in place, and the thick garment slid off his back like a wet seal. A slight shake of his head sent his dark slouch hat flying. All three guards gasped in surprise. Standing square in the glare of their three flashlights was a tall, slender man dressed in a bright red Harlequin costume. From the tip of his cherry-red boots to the top of his crimson fool's crown, he wore only shades of red. Too late, the three security men realised he had used the momentary distraction of his costume to raise his gold flute to his mouth.

Two notes sounded. All three men dropped to the floor, unconscious.

"The Red Minstrel strikes again," said the crimson figure as he scurried up the marble stairs, two steps at a time. "Not that those three were much of a threat."

He found the Red Ruby of Mercury at the end of a lavish display hall on the building's second floor. The gem was encased in a six-inch-thick slab of bulletproof glass, surrounded by a random focus sapphire laser protection grid. The display was in the center of a ten-foot circle of pressure-sensitive tiles, set to drop the stone and its case into a steel vault beneath the floor if jolted by the weight of anything heavier than a mosquito. The protections, however, were designed to keep ordinary criminals at bay. They were useless against supervillains.

A series of three trills from the Minstrel's flute shattered every glass case in the hall, disabled the pressure-sensitive tiles, and melted the laser beam projector. Eagerly, the crimson-clad clown of chaos grabbed the magnificent gem with his free hand. Ever since he had read about the jewel a week before in the newspapers, he had known he must possess it. Like the fabled Olympus Diamond, the Mercury Ruby contained powers beyond human comprehension. Powers that were about to become his.

"Put down the rock, Minstrel!"

The Red Minstrel whirled. He recognised that voice. There, at the other end of the hall, stood a young black police officer dressed in a black-and-silver special forces uniform, his entire body surrounded by flame, and yet he didn't burn. Here was Officer Prometheus, the policeman superhero who the Minstrel's own chaos power had helped create.

"Ill met by moonlight, proud Prometheus," said the Red Minstrel. When confronted by unexpected peril, he liked quoting William Shakespeare. The bard's words were always so dramatic.

"Yeah, whatever," said the human inferno. "I was

patrolling the park when I noticed the doors on the Rose Center were gone. Didn't know exactly what was going on. It's always a treat for me to find my favorite lunatic at play."

"Perhaps a deal...." said the Minstrel, knowing he was wasting his breath.

"Not in this lifetime," answered Officer Prometheus. A fireball glowing in one hand, he took a step forward. "Put down the ruby. Now."

"Whatever you say, Officer," the Minstrel replied, giggling. He suddenly knew exactly what he had to do. The voices in his head, silent for most of the evening, were talking – instructing him, commanding him.

"Cry havoc," he recited as per their wishes and with a flick of the wrist, sent the gem flying into the air. "And let slip the dogs of war."

The Mercury Ruby dropped to the thickly carpeted floor a dozen feet away from the startled Prometheus. For an instant, the air in the Rose Center thrummed with unimaginable power. Lights flickered on and off throughout the building. Filaments of cold lightning swarmed across metal decorations. Soundlessly, from the ruby's center poured a swirling cloud of darkness. A silent tornado of black air, it twisted and turned and resolved itself into the shape of a man. A very big man clad only in steel-edged workboots and a pair of worn cutoff jeans. A glowing, heavily-muscled giant with bone-white skin, a shaved head, massive jet-black eyebrows that met over his nose, and sunken tiny yellow eyes. A huge man whose gnarled, bony hands were curled into fists the size of buckets.

"Who be ya?" he growled in a voice as deep as a mineshaft. "Where is me?"

The Red Minstrel blinked. The voices in his head were silent again, and they hadn't said a word about a genie. Still, he knew better than to ignore a gift from the Chaos Lords.

"You're in Empire City," he said, raising one arm and pointing at Officer Prometheus. "And that man's your enemy!"

"Don't listen to that…" began Prometheus.

His mistake was talking instead of moving. Three incredible, quick steps and the giant was on him. Fingers thick as steel cables wrapped around Prometheus's neck. With a jerk of sheer brute power, the giant raised the officer five feet into the air. Astonishingly, though Prometheus's mystic flames burned bright blue, the mystery man remained untouched by the fire.

"Ya ain't so tough," said the giant and without effort, tossed the policeman halfway down the hall.

Prometheus's body came to a crashing halt at the base of the far-left wall. The cop didn't move, and the Red Minstrel wondered if the young man was dead. Though he himself had tried more than once to end Prometheus's life, he considered the police officer his personal prey and didn't like it when outsiders intruded where they didn't belong. Not that he was stupid enough to say something like that to this mysterious mangler.

"That was quite…impressive," offered the Minstrel, then found himself unable to speak another word. The giant had him by the throat, thick fingers squeezing into his neck like a vise.

"Urk, urk," the Minstrel gurgled, waving his hands around, trying to signal the giant that they were on the same side. The big man's lips parted in a twisted grin.

"Naah," he said. "Don't need no stinkin' partners. Why share when you can have it all?"

A philosophy I can appreciate, the Red Minstrel concluded as everything went dark.

Five Days Later

"Any change in Prometheus's condition?" asked Adam Sinclair, looking down at the unmoving body of the policeman superhero sprawled lifelessly on the white sheets of the hospital bed. A dozen monitors and tubes were attached to the man's head, neck, and arms. They recorded his every movement, his every breath, his every heartbeat. But they offered no clue to his malady or explained why each day he sank further and further into a coma, the life-force mysteriously draining out of him. The same malady afflicted the other three metabeings lying paralysed and unconscious in the room: the diabolical Red Minstrel, the amazing Slipstream, and the greatest superhero of the modern era, the leader of the Guard, the man called Sentinel.

"A change? Nothing worth mentioning," said the attractive, dark-haired woman who was acting as nurse for the fallen metahumans. Though she possessed amazing homeopathic natural healing powers, nothing Mother Raven did seemed to help the unmoving trio. "Each day their vital signs grow weaker and weaker. Whatever malignancy is sucking the life out of them is beyond my skills, Caliburn."

Sinclair, who had fought evil for years under the name Caliburn, scowled. He preferred confronting his enemies face to face. His battles took place on the land, up in the clouds, under the sea. Not in an emergency ward in Empire City General.

"What about the ordinary citizens who've been stricken?" he asked, knowing he'd like the answer no better.

"The same story," said Mother Raven. The descendent of Native American Ojibwa chiefs, she spoke with a quiet, noble dignity that befit her proud heritage. "I feel terrible about them. Victims of circumstance. Punished for being at the wrong place at the wrong time. They remain in the same unnatural state, the life-energy dripping out of them one drop at a time. It's our duty to protect our fellow citizens, and this time we've failed. Unless we do something, they'll all be dead by the week's end."

The cell phone in Sinclair's pocket chirped once and began playing "God Save the Queen." He flipped open the receiver and pushed down the answer button. "Yes," he said, then fell silent. After a minute, he continued, "Yes, yes, we'll be right there," and hung up.

"Something important?" asked Mother Raven, picking up the subtle but definite change in Sinclair's attitude.

"That was Red Phoenix," replied Sinclair. "Remember that strange character we met during our last encounter with the Red Minstrel? He wore a mask and called himself Drifter?"

"I remember," said Mother Raven. "Why?"

"He just showed up at the tower, claiming he knows what's happening to Prometheus, Sentinel, and all the others. More important, he thinks he knows how to save them."

"I'm gone," said Mother Raven and tapped her raven staff on the floor. She vanished, leaving nothing more than a trace of a shadow. Sinclair smiled. Raven knew how to travel! It would take him fifteen minutes in rush-hour traffic to return to the Guard's headquarters in the Olympian Tower. At least Raven and Phoenix wouldn't try anything without his approval. He was, with Sentinel and Slipstream laid low, temporary commander of the Guard.

Titular leader or not, when he finally arrived at the tower, both Raven and Phoenix looked at him in annoyance.

"This is an emergency," said Phoenix. "Considering the urgency of the situation, you could have changed into your armour and arrived here quicker."

"Ladies, ladies," he said, raising his hands in a gesture of peace. "I needed a few minutes, mingling incognito with the ordinary people of this city, to strengthen my inner resolve. After all, they're the ones we're fighting for. That's something we must never forget."

Caliburn turned to the man seated at the opposite side of the round table.

Drifter wore a long, brightly colored coat and several scarves. All were patterned with vivid purples, blues, and greens, with a dab of silver. A dimension mask covered most of his head. A leather cap, it sported huge goggles, like those worn by 1920s aviators.

"Drifter, good to see you again," Caliburn declared, though he instantly felt foolish for his choice of words. In most situations, Drifter wasn't really seen by anyone. His features remained hidden to all but his closest friends. "You know something about these attacks?"

"I think so," said Drifter. His voice was plain, if just a bit odd, like his clothing. He had the slightest of accents, but from where, Caliburn couldn't say. "Before coming here, I went to the Rose Center, the college conference room where Slipstream had been giving his speech when he was stricken, and the ice rink where Sentinel was ambushed – everywhere the monster has struck up to now. I did some investigating. All three locations were monitored by video cameras, yet at all three spots, the tapes were blank."

"We know that," said Caliburn. "Just as we know that the three guards at the Rose Center, the fourteen professors at the conference, and the eighty-two children and adults at the skating arena had absolutely nothing in common other than their presence at those places. We're not entirely inept…"

"I'm not trying to cast aspersions on your deductive pow-ers," said Drifter. "I know firsthand how difficult it is dealing with disaster when it affects your friends or family. You've done everything possible for the victims. I meant no disre-spect. The problem is that you're not capable of locating – much less defeating – this monster. None of us are."

"None of us?" repeated Red Phoenix. "Why do you say that?"

"We're all products of this world, this universe," said Drifter, rising to his feet. He stood over six feet tall and with his overcoat, scarves, and mask, was a striking figure. "As such, we can fight any enemy from this dimension. But this foe – he's from another. I suspect he is some sort of vampiric entity, one capable of draining the life-essence from our real-ity. And if Slipstream and Sentinel couldn't stop him, we must consider the possibility that he's beyond the reach of our metapowers. Just as his image refused to register on the video tapes."

"An inter-dimensional monster?" said Red Phoenix. "You mean a killer from a parallel universe, like the invaders from the Dark Empire? We were able to use our powers against them."

"Not all worlds of the space-time continuum – the totality of universes we call the multiverse – obey the same laws of physics as ours," replied Drifter. "In some parallel realities, for example, there are three laws of thermodynamics instead of the usual two. We got lucky with the dimension of the Dark Empire. This time, we're not.

"When I visited the three crime scenes, I sensed an eerie, unstable form of psychic energy unlike anything I've ever encountered before. The horror preying on Empire City is an outsider, a monster from another reality. Probably a criminal summoned by the Red Minstrel. Once here, he turned on him, as well. There's nothing we can do to stop this being. He's invulnerable to our powers."

"We're helpless?" said Mother Raven. "I can't accept that."

"Nor can I," said Caliburn. "Maybe there's nothing we can do to stop this fiend, but I refuse to surrender without a fight."

"Surrender?" said Drifter, spreading his arms wide. "Who said anything about surrendering?"

"But, you…" began Red Phoenix.

"*We* can't defeat this monster," said Drifter. "That doesn't mean someone else – someone from another reality – can't."

"Okay, Drifter," said Caliburn. "You've got my attention…"

"Somehow, someway, the Red Minstrel opened a gateway between dimensions and summoned this psychic monster into our reality," said Drifter. "I possess the ability to walk between universes and bring things back from them. I always thought returning with someone capable of solving a specific problem might be possible. It seems like now is the time to find out if I was right."

"I'm not sure I follow your reasoning," said Mother Raven. "How do you know you'd find the right person to fight this energy-devouring monster?"

"And locate someone who'd be willing to risk their life

doing so?" added Red Phoenix.

"When I concentrate on finding something special," said Drifter, "and I walk the ghost winds, I return with what I need. I'm not sure myself how my power works. All I know is that I find what I need. I'm certain that if I search for help in this fight, I'll find someone."

"Then it sounds to me like the decision's been made," said Caliburn. "Nothing we do in life is without some risk. People are dying, and we have to try to save them. Since Drifter's plan is the only one on the table, I say we accept his offer. Agreed?"

"Agreed," said Red Phoenix.

"Agreed," said Mother Raven.

"Good," said Drifter. "Then excuse me, won't you? There's no time like the present."

Without another word, he was gone.

"That was rather sud…" began Red Phoenix. Before he could finish the thought, Drifter popped back into existence a few feet away from where he had just been standing.

But he was no longer alone.

Red Phoenix gasped in surprise. Not only had Drifter emerged an instant after he had disappeared, he'd brought someone with him: a woman, slender and attractive, wearing a coal-black sheath dress, a diamond necklace with matching diamond earrings, and five-inch stiletto heels. She had long black hair with a hint of purple running through the strands. In one hand she held a small black evening bag, in the other a black walking stick with a finely engraved silver handle. She definitely did not look like a crime fighter. In fact, she reminded Red Phoenix, who liked to go to the movies, of a certain dark-haired young actress who had recently married a much older star.

The woman stood perfectly still, only turning her head slightly to take in the whole of the room and the costumed figures in it. Her dark eyes showed no signs of panic, and, after a few seconds, her full red lips curled into a lazy smile. "This definitely isn't the League of Women Voters Charity Ball."

"Excuse me," said Caliburn, the slightest frown on his face. He had been expecting someone quite different. But like all superheroes, he adapted quickly to surprise. "My friend was searching the dimensions for someone who could aid us in a perilous battle with the forces of evil. Are you that person?"

"Forces of evil, huh?" said the woman. She twisted her head, as if pondering Caliburn's words. "This obviously isn't Oz. Nor Barsoom, judging from the gravity. The pollution's familiar. Early twenty-first century America, I'd guess. And you four must be the guardians of the city?"

"The Guard," said Red Phoenix. In her armour, she towered above the stranger. "We're the Guard of Empire City."

"Right," said the stranger. "*Empire City*. It's not Gotham City, not Metropolis, not Center City, not downtown L.A., not the streets of San Francisco, not Genosha, and definitely not the City at the Edge of Forever. Interesting."

"She remind you of that movie actress?" whispered Mother Raven, stepping next to Red Phoenix. "You know, the one who was in that musical? The one who does all those TV ads for long-distance plans and hand cream…?"

"Look here, Miss…?" began Caliburn.

"Taine," said the stranger. "Ms. Sydney Taine."

"All right, then, Ms. Taine. We really don't have any time for delays. People are dying in Empire City. Friends of ours, as well as innocent bystanders. We have to help them. So I need the truth. Our friend here pulled you out of your dimension because he sensed that you could help us. Can you or can't you?"

"I'm not sure," replied Sydney Taine. She took a step forward. "At least not until I hear all the details. Do you mind if I sit down? And maybe could I get a drink?"

"Of course," said Mother Raven. She acted as the Guards' unofficial hostess whenever they had visitors. "What would you like?"

"A martini, perhaps?" said Taine, settling into a seat at the round table.

"If you like," replied Mother Raven. "Rather early in the day for alcohol, isn't it?"

"Fifteen minutes ago, it was midnight for me," said Taine. "Still, you're right. Do you have diet soda?"

"A Diet Jooki?" asked Mother Raven.

"Fine."

Taine seemed honest enough, but Red Phoenix wasn't totally convinced the stranger was on the side of truth and justice. For her, action spoke lots louder than words. She intended to keep a close watch on Ms. Taine.

"You seem to be adjusting rather well to the whole concept of dimension displacement," said Drifter, sitting on the table's edge. He drummed his fingers nervously. "Most people are stunned when they discover that parallel worlds actually exist. Much more so when they learn that humans can travel between them."

"I'm not most people," said Taine, taking a sip from the tall, frosted glass of Diet Jooki brought to her by Mother Raven. As usual, Raven had brought each of them a glass of chilled grapefruit juice along with a tray of carrot sticks, crackers, and a veggie dip. "I possess a very open mind," Taine concluded. "Now, tell me this problem with the forces of evil."

Forty minutes later, Caliburn finished the story. As with everything he did, Adam Sinclair was extremely thorough. Even Red Phoenix, who was fascinated by small details, couldn't think of a thing to add.

"Interesting," said Taine, "very interesting. Tell me, was anything missing from the scene of the first attack?"

"A gem," said Red Phoenix. This was her area of expertise. "A mysterious jewel known as the Red Ruby of Mercury. The ruby's full history is unknown, but this exhibition was the first time it had ever been displayed in public."

"Hmmm," said Caliburn. "The Red Minstrel has some priors involving rare gems, does he not, Phoenix?"

"The Olympus Diamond," answered Red Phoenix. "He stole it from the Temple of Mars about ten years ago. The jewel evidently boosted his powers. In a very short time, he went from smalltime thief to criminal mastermind."

"This Olympus Diamond – what happened to it?"

"It's downstairs, encased in plastic and secured in a lead box in our trophy room," said Red Phoenix. "The Minstrel grew careless, and the last time we fought, the Guard seized it from him. It's been in our possession ever since."

"Snap, crackle, pop," said Sydney Taine. "It's all starting to fall into place. There's only one more mystery that needs examining. I need to see your fallen comrades. Is it possible for us to visit the hospital?"

"Of course," replied Mother Raven. "Anything that will help."

"Then let's go." Sydney Taine rose to her feet in a swift, fluid motion that Phoenix found impressive. This woman was more than she appeared. "I'm the impatient type. I don't like waiting around."

"I'll call Doctor Drake," said Mother Raven. "I'll ask him to bend a few rules."

In the special ward set up for the victims of this latest disaster to strike Empire City, Taine walked from victim to victim, studying each one for a few seconds, then moving on. She moved with a feline stealth that Red Phoenix couldn't help but admire, especially since Taine still wore five-inch stiletto heels. Staying balanced in high heels was a talent neither Phoenix, nor her alter ego, Sarah, had ever mastered. She stuck to magic boots and oxfords.

"Any clues?" she asked Taine when the mystery woman finished her rounds.

"Maybe," said Taine. "I'll know better in a minute."

Taine twisted her left hand in a motion that Phoenix found impossible to follow. Some movements were unworkable in three dimensions and Phoenix felt certain Taine had just performed one. The young woman's hand had been empty a second ago. Now, between thumb and fingers, she held a thick paperbound book.

"How did you…?" began Phoenix. Her own Phoenix

Blade was of mystic origins, but sorcery still made her wary.

"Trade secret," said Taine. "I need to look up some stuff. How about finding the others? They wandered off looking for Doctor Drake. By the time you get them, I should be ready to leave."

Feeling somewhat bemused, Red Phoenix went in search of her companions. Being the only superheroes in the hospital, they weren't difficult to locate. Drifter, despite wearing goggles with glass lenses thick as the bottoms of old pop bottles, obviously noticed something was wrong.

"What's bothering you, Phoenix?" he asked as the four of them headed back to the emergency ward.

"It's Ms. Taine," said Phoenix, all of her anxieties and suspicions bubbling to the surface. "She's too calm, too collected for everything that's happening. She's not surprised by anything we say, and she's too confident about what she's doing. And she pulled some sort of guide book out of thin air a minute ago."

"A book?" repeated Mother Raven, sounding puzzled. "At least it wasn't a gun. Book people are usually good people."

"What if it's a tome of black magic?" said Red Phoenix, her temper rising. Sometimes Mother Raven was incredibly naive. "A grimoire?"

"Well," said Drifter, "I brought her here. I guess it's up to me to ask her the tough questions."

That proved to be less traumatic than anyone imagined. Taine was seated on the edge of Sentinel's bed, waiting for them. She held the thick, paperbound book, open to the middle, in her hands. Before Drifter could say a word, the dark-haired woman started talking.

"You're all obviously wondering about me. I can see it in your eyes, your expressions. Well, I can't say much. It's not allowed. Just remember this: Drifter went searching for a solution to your problem, and he came up with me. He didn't make a mistake."

"Implying," said Caliburn, who liked things spelled out in black and white, "that he was meant to find you?"

"Perhaps," said Taine, with a smile. "The multiverse consists of billions and billions of alternate realities. Separated by quantum steps, they normally don't intersect. A few gifted individuals – people like Drifter – possess the power to walk the ghost winds, the path between worlds. Fortunately, most of the gifted are harmless, or even helpful.

"However, there's also a group called the Others. A melange of maniacs, madmen, and psychopaths possessing incredible psychic powers, they stay strong by devouring life-forces as they travel throughout the multiverse. They're also quite keen on getting their hands on the Chaos Gems, fabled stones of power, possession of which will give them control over all creation."

"The Red Ruby of Mercury," said Phoenix, hardly realising she was speaking.

"Exactly," said Taine. "As with the Olympus Diamond. The Red Minstrel somehow unleashed the power of the ruby and summoned one of the Others to your world. He's the cosmic vampire who's feeding on the life-energy of the people he's encountered during the past week. He'll continue to do so until he's stopped. I did some research and identified the monster responsible for these crimes. He's big and mean, and he's called the Eradicator. I take it you've figured out already that he's immune to all your powers. And you were right to get me, too, because he's not immune to mine. You see, I guard the multiverse…"

"For whom?" asked Caliburn.

"That's not for me to reveal," said Taine. She rose to her feet, twisted her hands in a fourth-dimensional gesture, and the book disappeared. "Let's get back to Guard headquarters. It's time for me to change into my fighting gear."

"You plan to battle this monster tonight?" said Red Phoenix. Much as she was trying not to like this beautiful woman, she couldn't help but admire Taine's intensity.

"There's no time like the present," answered Taine, sounding very much like Drifter for a moment. "Besides, once we take the Olympus Diamond out of that lead-lined box, the Eradicator will sense its power. He'll come looking for it. I'd better be waiting."

In all of her years as a hero, Mother Raven had to admit she'd never seen an outfit quite like Sydney Taine's. It wasn't that the clothing showed much skin. It didn't. Compared to the skimpy red halter top and lowrider yellow stretch pants worn by Red Phoenix, Taine's garb made her look positively overdressed. It wasn't what she wore as much as how she wore it that made an impression.

Tightly-stretched black leather clung to Taine's every curve, from her shapely neck to her taut, perfect breasts, down past her narrow waist, long legs, to her small, well-defined toes. The only break in black was a silver zipper that started at the hollow of her neck and descended to her navel. On her feet Taine wore black, five-inch spike heels.

"Isn't your outfit somewhat…constraining?" asked Mother Raven as Sydney fiddled with her make-up in front of a mirror. Raven had volunteered her quarters for Taine to dress while Red Phoenix, Drifter, and Caliburn went downstairs to the trophy room for the Olympus Diamond.

"It's like a second skin," said Taine, digging through her makeup kit searching for something. The kit, like the garment bag that held Sydney's costume, came out of nowhere with a four-dimensional twist of the wrist. More than anything else, that trick had convinced Caliburn that Taine was the real deal. "Besides," she concluded with a smile, "wearing leather gives me a rush."

"But the material's so tight. How can you wear underwear beneath it?"

"Underwear?" said Sydney with a laugh. "You're kidding, of course."

Raven opened her mouth to say something, but the words didn't emerge. She only hoped she wasn't blushing.

"All done," declared Sydney a minute later. "What do you think?"

Mother Raven didn't know what to say. Taine had pulled

her long hair up to the center of her head, tied it there, and then teased the long strands outward to form a gigantic puff-ball of black and purple above her scalp. Purple eyeliner and eyelashes accentuated the hair color, and purple-white lipstick completed the fashion statement. Though not an expert on club clothing, Mother Raven still thought Taine's look was very much in the neopunk-goth-spiky-carrot tradition. It was a compliment Taine accepted with good graces.

"It's an outfit designed to attract attention," said Taine. Holding her silver-handled walking stick in one hand, she waved the cane about like a sword. "I think I'm all set. Hopefully the others will be ready in the arena with the diamond."

They were. The arena was a five-story-high gymnasium in Guard headquarters that normally held a boxing ring in the center and all sorts of athletic and track equipment everywhere else. Tonight it had been completely cleared. A stand had been set toward the back of the arena, and resting on it was the uncased Olympus Diamond. The jewel throbbed with force, and unseen winds swirled around its stand.

Positioned behind the stand were the three Guard members and Drifter. They knew their powers were of little use against the Eradicator, but they also knew that should Taine fall, they wouldn't surrender the diamond without a fight.

"You sure this maniac will sense the diamond and come searching for it?" asked Caliburn. "He hasn't surfaced from whatever hellhole he's been hiding in for the last two nights."

"He'll come," said Taine. "His kind senses cosmic energy. I'm sure he's probably on the way here as we speak. Time for last minute instructions."

"What kind of instructions?" asked Red Phoenix, sounding suspicious. Raven understood Phoenix's concern. Usually, it was their enemies who wore provocative clothing, not their allies. Taine was almost too beautiful not to be bad.

"My fighting style is known as *capoeira*," said Taine as she walked through several quick ballet stretching exercises that involved bending her body into pretzel shapes. Afterward, balancing on one leg, she raised the other leg straight up in the air, pointing her toes to the ceiling. Then she repeated the maneuver with limbs reversed. "Where I come from, it was invented by African slaves in Brazil over two hundred years ago. It's a combination of martial arts and dance. When performed properly, it's quite deadly."

"You're that good?" asked Drifter.

"Definitely," replied Taine. "Still, the situation isn't so simple. The Eradicator is siphoning life-energy from your fallen comrades and the hundred-plus people in the hospital ward. That's going to make him extremely powerful. The only chance I have to beat him is to channel some equally strong life-force. *Yours*."

Red Phoenix raised her sword to shoulder height. "And how do you plan to do that?"

"Through song," said Taine. "When *capoeirista's* battle, they're usually surrounded by a circle of people known as a *roda*. The fighter recites the first verse of a *chula*, a chant, and the crowd responds with the chorus. The ritual repeats again and again, creating a basic form of cosmic energy, *orisha*, that fuels the *capoeirista's* movements. It's simple but effective."

"So for you to defeat the Eradicator, you need us to chant the chorus of this song," said Mother Raven. "Actually, this custom sounds quite similar to the war dances my people hold the night before battle."

"Close enough," said Taine as the arena floor rumbled. Alarm bells rang all through the tower. Something massive and very evil approached. "The verse is simple: 'I am the elder who learns; I am the child who teaches.' Sing as loud as you like. The greater the enthusiasm, the stronger the *orisha*. And I have a feeling I'm going to need all the cosmic energy I can get."

Caliburn turned away, muttering, "I'm British. We never sing in public..."

Taine opened her mouth to reply, but the words were drowned out by the middle pair of doors to the gym crashing off their hinges. Standing in the opening was the Other called the Eradicator.

The heroes of the Guard had never before sensed such raw, threatening physical power. The Eradicator was a giant of a man, nearly seven feet tall, with shoulders five feet across and arms that nearly reached to the floor. His massive barrel chest was white as chalk and covered with muscles. In one giant hand, he held a five-foot-long piece of steel pipe. It looked like a twig.

"Gimme da jewel," he said, his voice rumbling like an earthquake. "And I won't hurtcha'…much."

"Come and get it, big man," replied Taine. "If you can."

"Ain't never been stopped by nobody," said the Eradicator as he stepped into the arena. "Not gonna be stopped now by some babe in leather, that be for sure."

"Talk, talk," said Taine. She executed a series of perfect walkover flips to bring herself within a few feet of the giant. "I'm not impressed."

"Graah," snarled the Eradicator and snatched at Sydney's right shoulder with his huge left hand. Dropping to her knees, she spun to the outside and thrust her walking stick straight into the big man's underarm. It was a blow that would have paralysed an ordinary person's side; the monster hardly seemed to notice.

With deceptive speed, the giant slammed his other hand at Taine's midriff. Moving equally fast, she backflipped away – only to be caught by a roundhouse slap from the Eradicator's left hand. With an audible *thunk*, the blow sent her sprawling a dozen feet to the side.

The big man glanced toward the Olympus Diamond, then shook his head and turned toward Taine. She was just getting to her feet when he charged, arms outstretched to trap her in his grasp.

"Watch out!" cried Mother Raven, but Taine needed no warning.

Sydney jumped forward and up, her body arching over the Eradicator's head in a perfect midair somersault. Landing on her feet, she twirled and slapped her walking stick against the back of one of the giant's knees. The big man grunted in surprise but otherwise showed no pain.

"No man exists without some terrors," Taine proclaimed loudly as the Eradicator spun about to confront her once again.

It took Mother Raven a second to realise that Sydney's words were the start of her chant. "I am the elder who learns; I am the child who teaches," she answered, trying to catch the same rhythm as Taine.

"I hate dem singin'," said the Eradicator, swinging his left fist in a monstrous uppercut capable of crushing bones. Taine pinwheeled to the side and snapped her stick across the giant's fingers. The blow left a bright red mark.

"A big man falls, it sounds like thunder," chanted Sydney.

Like a crashing tidal wave, the Eradicator leapt forward. He seemed intent on catching Taine between his arms and crushing her. Tapping his forehead with the silver tip of her walking stick, she half-slid, half-danced out of his grasp.

"I am the elder who learns," sang Mother Raven, slapping Caliburn on the side of the head. The Englishman hadn't made a sound since the fight started. "I am the child who teaches."

"A good man fights his terrors," chanted Taine as she nimbly skipped around the Eradicator, using her walking stick to jab him a half-dozen times in the stomach and waist. She seemed to be gaining strength and speed with each verse of her song.

"I am the elder who learns," sang Mother Raven along with Caliburn. The masked Brit sounded somewhat stiff and formal, but his voice was loud and clear. "I am the child who teaches," responded Red Phoenix and Drifter.

"Gotcha!" bellowed the Eradicator. Both his hands fastened on Taine's shoulders. "Now you're mine."

"A bad man is much too stupid," chanted Taine and slammed her cane right between the Eradicator's eyes. The giant groaned and stumbled backward, but his huge hands still held Taine by the shoulders.

"I am the elder who learns," sang the four superhumans

at the top of their voices. The rafters of the arena seemed to shake from the sound. Using the first and second fingers of her left hand, Taine jabbed the Eradicator in the eyes. The Other howled, dropped Taine, and bent his head, both hands clutching his face.

"I am the child who teaches," chanted Mother Raven, Red Phoenix, Caliburn, and Drifter as Taine whacked the Eradicator with her walking stick behind his right ear.

The giant crashed to the arena floor, unconscious. Just to be sure, Taine hit him three more times on the skull. The Eradicator didn't move.

All four metas ran over as the woman in black leather reached outside of space and produced a gigantic set of man-acles that she immediately slapped onto the Eradicator's wrists.

"The cuffs will break this monster's hold on your friends and the innocents," said Taine. "Plus keep him manageable until I drop him off in his new home."

"New home?" repeated Drifter.

"For violating Section 7, Article 5679 of the Multiverse Civil Code, I hereby sentence the Eradicator to fifty years of running for his life in the Dimension of Giant Sand Beetles," said Taine, sounding very dignified. "I'm not only a guardian of the multiverse, but I'm a judge and jury, as well."

"How can we ever thank you?" asked Caliburn.

"Don't thank me," said Taine, reaching down and grab-bing the chains imprisoning the Eradicator's hands. "Thank yourselves. Without you sacrificing some of your dignity to chant my *chula*, I'd never have defeated this monster."

The cell phone in Caliburn's pocket chirped. Pulling the phone free, he flipped it on and listened for an instant.

"Sentinel and the others have awakened," he announced. He paused as the voice on the other end spoke again. "But the Red Minstrel's already gone."

"That's my cue to leave, as well," said Taine. "Don't worry about my clothes and stuff. They'll follow me home. They always do."

Then, without another word, she was gone. As was the Eradicator.

"Such an interesting woman," said Drifter. "And possessing a power much like mine. It's too bad we hardly got to talk."

"Don't worry, my friend," said Mother Raven. "Somehow, I have the feeling we'll be seeing Ms. Sydney Taine again."

◆┈┈➤

THE APOCALYPSE QUATRAIN

-1-

Someone was knocking on the door. Loudly. Groggily, Sidney Taine rolled over in bed and glanced at the clock on his nightstand. Four A.M. Not the usual time for visitors. Forcing himself awake, Taine pulled on his robe and headed for the door. The pounding continued relentlessly.

Taine peered out the peephole into the hallway. As a private detective specializing in cases too bizarre, too unusual for other investigators to handle, he had made more than his share of enemies. It never hurt to be careful, though it seemed doubtful anyone seeking revenge would announce his presence by knocking.

Two big, burly men in trench coats stood in the corridor. Taine didn't recognize either of them, but he knew their type. Government agents.

"You gentlemen looking for me?" he asked, opening the door.

"Sidney Taine?" replied the taller of the two.

"That's me."

"Your government needs you, Mr. Taine," said the other man, pulling out his wallet and flashing an identification card. Taine hardly bothered looking at it. "Would you please get dressed? Immediately."

"I take it the government can't wait till morning," said

Taine. He wasn't surprised when the agent shook his head. "Come on in. It will take me a few minutes to put on some clothes."

"Dress warm," advised the first man. "It's pretty damned cold where you're going."

The agent wasn't exaggerating. Three hours later, Taine climbed out of a military jet onto a landing strip in the middle of nowhere. A howling wind roared off the desolate, empty plains. The cold hit Taine like a hammer, chilling him to the bone. He guessed he was somewhere in the Dakotas, but if someone told him it was actually the ancient Norse hell, he would not have disagreed.

A half-dozen men in army uniforms escorted him to the only buildings in sight, a handful of concrete huts that barely broke the surface of the prairie. Taine wasn't surprised to discover that there was nothing inside the blockhouses other than elevators leading beneath the surface. Wordlessly, the soldiers put him in one and pressed the down button. The forty seconds it took at high speed to reach the bottom told the detective all he needed to know about how big and how important the base was buried beneath the frozen ground.

A familiar figure waited for him when the elevator door opened to a bustling underground complex. "General Parker," said Taine, smiling. "I should have guessed you were behind this abduction."

"Good to see you again, Taine," said Parker, advancing with hand outstretched. "Sorry for all the mystery. We required a man of your talents, and there wasn't time for long explanations. So we sent out the hounds. Thank God they found you."

A short, stocky man with bright red cheeks and a thick mane of shockingly white hair, Parker was the Army's top man in the Midwest. Taine had met him the year before when the general's son disappeared under unusual circumstances. The detective's unique grounding in the occult had enabled him to find the boy when all others failed.

They shook hands. The general's grip was as firm as ever,

but his arm trembled either from fatigue or worry. Taine suspected it was a combination of both. Something important was going on that frightened the officer, and Parker was not a man who scared easily.

"Come with me," said the general. "The others are waiting for us in the conference room. Did you eat breakfast? I can have some food sent over from the mess hall."

"Black coffee will be fine," said Taine. "Exactly what is this place, General? With the Soviet Union gone, I thought secret bases like this no longer existed."

Parker smiled briefly as they walked down a long, white corridor. Dozens of men and women, in both uniforms and civilian clothing, hurried past them, rushing from place to place like rats in a gigantic maze.

"You're at the hub of the North American Early Defense System, Taine. It's a self-contained fortress with links to all the major missile and chemical weapon networks on the continent. There's a similar base located a few miles outside of Washington, D.C. As envisioned by its creators, one or the other stronghold is where the major battles of the next war were to be fought and won. Fortunately, that prospect no longer seems probable.

"Officially, this base no longer exists. All our records indicated that it, and the one in Washington, were dismantled shortly after the implementation of various treaties signed during the past ten years. We lied, of course, as did the Russians. Neither of us fooled the other. Now they've truly retired from the game; we're the only player left. But there's plenty of others on the sidelines waiting to deal themselves in.

"The Cold War may be over, Taine, but that doesn't mean we can relax our defenses. World conditions are more volatile than when the Soviets were the only perceived threat. There's too many unfriendly nations with nuclear weapons capabilities. Communism might be dead, but it's been replaced by rabid nationalism and religious fanaticism. To be frank, I'm not sure the Cold War wasn't preferable to what we're faced with in its place."

The general ushered the detective into a large meeting room. A dozen people sitting at a U-shaped table awaited their arrival. Parker walked to an empty chair at the front of the room and motioned for Taine to take the seat next to him. As soon as the detective slid into place, an orderly brought him a cup of black coffee. Parker insisted on efficiency. Taine knew if the general specifically wanted him here, there had to be a good reason. Which meant it involved his knowledge of the supernatural and the occult.

"Mr. Taine is here at my invitation. I have dealt with him before and know something of his unique skills. He may be our only hope. Please speak freely to him. We don't have much time left. Dr. Silas, will you begin?"

Silas, a tall shadow of a man, completely bald, wearing glasses with lenses the thickness of pop bottle glass, rose to his feet. He did not look happy. They all looked as if they were waiting for a bomb to explode. On a base of this importance, the thought was a frightening one.

"Yesterday afternoon, during a routine camera scan of technicians serving the NAEDS mainframe computer, a programmer was observed feeding unauthorized information into the machine's memory banks. When confronted by security personnel, the man, Alan Wetherby, reacted violently and had to be subdued by force. Fortunately, he was not injured, and we were able to question him. He made no attempt to hide what he had done, and later interrogations using truth drugs confirmed what he told us. Actually, he seemed quite proud of his accomplishments."

Though it was chilly in the meeting room, Dr. Silas wiped off beads of sweat dripping down his forehead. "Wetherby had experienced a number of personal and emotional disasters during the past few years. His mother and father died in a car crash; his wife left him for another man; and his only child, a daughter, died from a drug overdose. Under such intense pressure, he turned not to religion, which he thought was a sham, but instead to mysticism. He found comfort in the obscure prophecies of the famous 16th century physician and seer, Michel de Nostradamus."

Taine grimaced. "He wasn't..."

"Unfortunately, he was," answered Dr. Silas. "For the past three months, Mr. Wetherby secretly fed the prophecies of Nostradamus into the NAEDS Base Computer. As far as we can tell, he managed to enter all but the last few quatrains into the mainframe's memory core."

"Why wasn't he caught earlier?"

"Good question. I've repeated it a thousand times myself. I don't have an answer, though. Outwardly, Wetherby acted normal. He worked on the NAEDS project for more than ten years and had the highest security clearance. Until he was apprehended, there was no reason to be suspicious of him. Needless to say, we are revising our psychological screening tests. But in this case, the damage is already done."

"Thank you, Doctor," said General Parker, nodding the man back to his seat. "Major Watkins, would you continue?"

Watkins spoke in quiet, measured tones, but fear echoed in his every word. "My department handles computer repairs and debugging. As soon as we understood what Wetherby had done, my team attempted to retrieve and eliminate the extraneous data from the core. It was then that we learned the full extent of our problem."

Watkins took a deep breath, as if about to plunge into a lake of ice water. "The NAEDS computer resisted all efforts to modify the core memory. Wetherby entered the prophecies as Class 1 priority transmissions. That classified the documents as wartime security information. The mainframe thus treated the prophecies as fact, not fancy.

"The computer, following standard defense procedures, immediately went on full alert, isolating its functions from any outside interference. Since that time, it has proceeded with actions we can only deem extremely dangerous to our national well-being. We can still communicate with the machine, but it refuses to answer any of our questions. Instead, it continues to print out four lines of verse I am told form one of the quatrains."

Watkins passed a sheet of paper to Taine. The detective scanned the page. Someone had scribbled on the top of the sheet, *Century X, Quatrain 74.*

> *The year of the great seventh number accomplished,*
> *It will appear at the time of the games of slaughter:*
> *Not far from the great millennial age,*
> *When the buried will go out from their tombs.*

The blood drained out of Taine's face as he read the passage. Now he understood why the general and his staff were so worried. They were staring at the end of the world and wanted him to tell them it wasn't true.

"What actually can the computer do?" Taine asked, wanting to make sure he wasn't assuming too much.

"The NAEDS computer is designed to wage all-out war in case of an enemy attack. If, as it seems to be the case, the machine believes we are involved in a war, it is capable of launching physical and chemical retaliation against the aggressors, wherever they may be in the world."

"Can't the president...?"

"The NAEDS mainframe was conceived to be our country's final line of defense if the president and Congress were unable to act. If, for example, they had been wiped out in the first enemy assault. It is a fully functional, standalone, defensive battle system, probably the most advanced computer network ever constructed. And as best we can determine, it is insane."

"The quatrain, Taine," said General Parker, "you're familiar with it?"

The detective rose to his feet and raised his voice loud enough so everyone in the room could hear him. There was no reason to hide the bad news. "It's known among students of the occult as The Apocalypse Quatrain."

Taine paused, deciding what to say next. The direct approach was best. "Nostradamus wrote his prophecies in no particular order, but most scholars agree if they were arranged in sequence, this particular one would be very close to the end. It describes the coming of Armageddon."

"The language seems pretty obscure," said the general. "Would the verse make any sense to the NAEDS mainframe?"

"That depends on how sophisticated a library the computer possesses and whether it can access the necessary information. From what Major Watkins stated, I suspect I know the answer to both queries."

"One of the prime functions of the NAEDS systems is logical analysis of information from a variety of sources," declared the major glumly. "Its memory bank contains the contents of the entire Library of Congress."

"Which, I feel certain," said Taine, "includes The Bible, and therefore, The Book of Revelation. Since most scholars feel that the book provided Nostradamus' inspirations for this verse, I think we must assume the meaning of the verse is clear to the computer. And from what you have told me, it is acting on that information."

"Please explain," said General Parker, his voice a whisper of dread.

"*The year of the great seventh number accomplished* does not refer to a specific date, but instead is a direct reference to the Book of Revelation. Seven appears throughout the text – there are seven stars, seven angels, seven trumpets, seven plagues, seven seals, seven vials of wrath. The most important is the seven plagues – including earthquakes, pestilence, wars, and such – which would all occur in one year, signifying the coming Apocalypse. Considering recent human history, that year is now.

"*It will appear at the time of the games of slaughter,*" continued Taine, "refers to a period of many wars. Need I mention the outbreaks of fighting in Europe, Asia, and elsewhere?"

The room was silent as he recited the next line. "*Not far from the great millennial age.* We are only a few years away from the new millennium."

Taine's voice echoed hollow in the chamber. "The last

line presents the inevitable conclusion. *When the buried will go out from their tombs.* Revelation again, with the dead returning to life at the Last Judgment."

"Or worse," said General Parker. "When we took our atomic missiles offline as per treaty agreements, we listed them as 'dead and buried.' Their silos became known as 'the tombs.' It appears that the NAEDS is attempting to fulfill the quatrain's prophecy. It is preparing the dead to go out from their tombs. And bring about the Final Apocalypse."

-2-

"You've informed the president?" asked Taine.

"He knows," said Parker. "He knows that the plotting of a lunatic believer in the prophecies of a sixteenth century astrologer threatens the entire world with nuclear destruction. But there's nothing he can do other than wait. And pray."

"Can't you shut off the computer's power supply? Or disconnect the weapon systems from it?"

"Don't you think we've tried all the obvious options?" Parker said angrily. He cooled off in seconds. "NAEDS is constructed to survive a major enemy assault. The computer mainframe has its own power source and is virtually invulnerable to a frontal attack. We could disable it and cut if off from the outside world in a week. But we don't have a week. According to our latest projections, the rearmed missile systems will be at full readiness in two more hours."

"Their targets?"

"Hundreds of locations in Europe and Asia. Every trouble spot in the past two centuries, and that covers just about all the major cities on both continents. We haven't been able to pinpoint each one, but if even a small percentage of the nuclear weapons explode, half the world will become a radioactive wasteland."

"Then there's only one question left to be answered," said Taine. "Why am I here? I'm not a military man or computer expert. How can I help?"

An attractive young woman rose to her feet. "We're hoping you can shut down the NAEDS computer on your own. Actually, we're praying. None of our other plans have worked. You're our last chance."

"Ms. Smythe is our computer guru," said General Parker. "She understands the NAEDS mainframe better than anyone. Her proposal is a long shot, but at this stage of the game, considering the stakes, I'm willing to gamble."

"What do you want me to do?" asked Taine.

"My scheme," said Ms. Smythe, "calls for someone who is extremely quick-witted, firmly grounded in mysticism and the occult, and can twist the truth to fit his own purposes. General Parker assures me that you fit the bill."

Taine smiled. "Close enough."

Ms. Smythe didn't smile back. "Everything hinges on the fact we can still communicate with the NAEDS mainframe. The machine listens to us but refuses to believe it is acting on erroneous information. The machine accepts the prophecies as truth. We can't change that. However, since the quatrains are so ambiguous, we're hoping that we can – you can – convince the computer there is more than one logical interpretation of the verse."

"What will that accomplish?"

"One of the basic differences between man and machine is that humans have the capability of accepting variable truths. In other words, we recognize that specific circumstances or facts do not always lead to the same conclusion. The laws of logic, of cause and effect, cannot be applied to human behavior."

A slight smile creased Ms. Smythe's lips. "We are creatures of emotion as well as logic. That is not the case with a computer. In its universe, if A implies B, and B implies C, then A must imply C. Every question has one answer, and one answer alone. The laws of mathematics and logic are fundamental and unyielding.

"Working with world events or battle scenarios, the mainframe can balance factors, evaluate possibilities, and come up with the most likely situation. However, we aren't dealing with actual happenings, but with the words of a man dead for centuries. The computer has settled on one specific meaning to the verse. We want you to provide it with another."

"I think I see where you're heading," said Taine. "If I can convince the mainframe its analysis of the quatrain is not the only logical explanation, that multiple solutions exist, the machine will be faced with a situation outside its frame of reference."

Ms. Smythe nodded. "Which, in theory, should throw its logic circuits into an unending memory loop, freezing the machine."

"In theory?" repeated Taine.

"We've never dealt with an insane computer before," said Ms. Smythe. "Nor one that believes in the prophecies of Nostradamus."

"Can you do it, Taine?" asked General Parker, his features grim.

The detective shrugged. "I wish the machine had picked another quatrain. Coming up with an alternative meaning is going to be a challenge. Especially considering the amount of time left. But I don't see that I have much choice. No choice at all."

-3-

Drawing in a deep breath, Taine opened his eyes and looked around. He stood on the edge of a huge stone cliff, a thousand feet above a raging, stormy sea. Monstrous waves, hundreds of feet high, crashed into the rock with incredible fury. Something immense and blood red, but otherwise vague, stirred in the center of the maelstrom.

Above him, thick crimson-tinted grey clouds swirled about angrily, stirred by powerful winds that ripped and tore at his clothing. Barely visible, in their heart was a mighty throne covered with emerald light. Before it burned seven torches of fire. Taine noted that no one sat in the great chair. Evidently, even the NAEDS computer had difficulty conceptualizing God.

Lightning flashed and thunder roared, and the world shook with the sound of hoof beats. Four gigantic horsemen approached, riding through the dark sky. The detective nodded as if in confirmation of his expectations.

He whispered to himself, "This isn't real. I'm sitting inside a communications booth hooked up to the mainframe by virtual reality software. It's how base personnel conduct business with the machine. Only now, I'm dealing with the computer's new persona." Mentally, he footnoted his last thought. "The *insane* computer's new persona."

The riders circled Taine, each of them the size of a small battleship. The first rode a pure white horse and carried a bow. He was the conqueror, and Taine expected he would speak for the group. The second, mounted on a red horse, carried a sword and brought war. The third, sitting on a black steed, carried a balance. The fourth rider, skeletal and clothed in a black robe, was Death, armed with a scythe, on a pale horse.

Taine knew them as the Four Horsemen of the Apocalypse, as described in Revelation. The chair in the heavens was the Throne of God, while the monster stirring in the sea was the Great Beast. Judging by the visible signs and portents, Taine concluded that the computer considered these moments the prelude to Armageddon. He adjusted his plans accordingly.

In his left ear, Ms. Smythe's voice whispered, "Thirty minutes to estimated missile launch." The miniature radio receiver was his only link to the real world.

"Who are you, mortal?" asked the white rider, his booming voice echoing through the night. "Why have you come here?"

"My name is Daniel," said Taine, the name of the most famous prophet of the Old Testament, whose visions helped shape Revelation. "I come seeking the truth."

"What truth?" asked the white rider, modulating its voice so it was no longer louder than normal speech.

According to most occult researchers, in a later section of Revelation, a rider on a white horse represented Christ resurrected. The implications of the computer's use of that figure as its spokesman disturbed Taine. Possibly the machine considered itself the instrument of God's will on Earth. It was not a comforting thought.

Taine closed his eyes for a second, marshalling his thoughts. Everything hinged on the next exchange. His gaze fixed on the white rider, the detective declared, "I search for understanding, for wisdom. What is the meaning of the Number of the Beast?"

"It is a human number," answered the white rider, the words coming directly from Revelation. "Its number is 666."

Inwardly, Taine breathed a sigh of relief. The dialogue had begun. None of the computer experts, including Ms. Smythe, knew for sure whether the mainframe in its battle alert mode would continue to answer questions directed to it. With that difficulty resolved, the detective could now proceed with sabotaging the machine.

"The number is 666," repeated Taine. "That confuses me. What then is the Great Seventh Number?"

"The dawning of the Apocalypse," said the white rider. "It is the time of seven seals, the seven angels, the seven gold bowls filled with the wrath of God, and the Beast with Seven Heads."

Taine smiled. The machine was drawing its information directly from Revelation. Considering the contradictory and obscure nature of that book, it was a dangerous practice – one that Taine fully intended to exploit.

"I don't understand," said Taine. "Nostradamus spoke of the year of the Great Seventh Number accomplished and said that it will appear. How can a time appear?"

The white rider hesitated before answering. "Nostradamus wrote in vague generalities and terms," the machine finally declared. "He was often poetic in speech."

"The Seventh Number," continued Taine, pressing his advantage. "Why didn't Nostradamus merely say seven if he meant that number? Isn't it likely that he was referring instead to the early Arabic practice of examining the whole numbers starting not with one but with zero? In that manner, all possible integers can be formed using combinations of single digits."

"It is possible," said the white rider, frowning.

"Using that assumption," said Taine, "the Seventh *Number* would actually be six. The Great Seventh Number thus becomes six multiplied. The year of the Great Seventh Number accomplished would therefore mean the year of Number 666. And since that is how the Great Beast is named in Revelation, it would clearly refer to the arrival of the Great Beast on Earth."

Taine realized his rationalization of the numbers was quite unorthodox. Still, he felt confident the computer would accept his reasoning, since binary, the heart of all computer language, was based on the use of zero as the first number.

Below, in the ocean, the thing at the heart of the maelstrom gained substance and shape. Though still partially hidden by the waters, the monster now had four heads. Taine didn't need a closer to look to know the creature possessed attributes of a leopard, bear, lion, and dragon. Or that one of its heads seemed to bear marks of a mortal wound that had healed. It was the Great Beast of the Apocalypse. The computer had revised its scenery.

"Isn't the Great Beast another name for Satan?" asked Taine. "Wasn't Satan, the Father of Lies, thrown into the sea where he rose again as the Beast?"

"That is correct," answered the computer, not realizing it had advanced another foot forward into Taine's trap.

"Another question puzzles me," said the detective. "What are games of slaughter?"

"War," answered the second rider, the bearer of the sword. "Men at war conduct games of slaughter."

"War?" repeated Taine, sounding dubious. "No man considers war a game. Doesn't the word games refer to pleasurable occupations?"

He paused dramatically. "Isn't man's greatest pleasure, sex, often called a game – the game of love? Is it possible that the games of slaughter refers instead to sex leading to death?"

The second rider shook his head. "That does not compute. Why would anyone engage in pleasurable behavior leading to extinction?"

"Nostradamus knew the answer," said Taine.

In his ear, Ms. Smythe's voice whispered, "Ten minutes and counting, Taine. Hopefully, you're making progress."

Using virtual reality to communicate directly to the computer cut Taine off completely with the outside world. General Parker, Ms. Smythe and the rest had no idea how he was progressing, and there was no way he could tell them. Obviously, his conversation so far had not caused the mainframe to delay the missile launching.

"Explain your remark," said the white rider.

"When the *buried* will go out from their *tombs*," said Taine, emphasizing the two words. "Nostradamus phrased his quatrains very carefully. He didn't say the dead would return to life, as in the Last Judgment. Instead, he spoke of the buried coming out of their tombs. The prophet wasn't describing some imaginary event. He was describing an actual event, something he witnessed himself. During his lifetime, men wrapped themselves up in shrouds and dwelled in their tombs. They were the buried who entered and departed their tombs."

Taine turned and pointed to the fourth rider, the one holding the scythe. "You know who I mean, don't you? They were your children."

The rider of the pale horse nodded. "Nostradamus lived during the time of the Black Death. In the plague years, many victims acted in just such a manner."

"A plague," said Taine. "The last line of the quatrain refers to a plague, not to the resurrection of the dead."

He spun around and confronted the white rider, now only a few feet away. In the blink of an eye, the four horsemen had shrunk down to mortal size. Below, the seas no longer churned, and the heavens above were silent.

"Five minutes," whispered Ms. Smythe.

"Century Ten, Verse 74, is not concerned with the end of the world," Taine said hurriedly, knowing time was running out. "Instead, it predicts the coming of a plague in the years leading up to the millennium, at the time of the Great Seventh Number accomplished. A plague we are experiencing right now. A plague brought about by sex that leads to death. A plague whose history is hidden in lies and deceit. A plague spread by behavior considered by fundamentalist Christians to be fostered by Satan, the Great Beast. *A plague called AIDS.*"

The riders were gone. As was their world. Taine stood facing a man who looked quite a bit like General Parker. They were in a meeting room similar to the one the detective had left an hour earlier.

"AIDS?" said the computer. "But...but..."

Blackness.

After a moment, Taine realized the virtual reality helmet was no longer functioning. In his ear, a very subdued Ms. Smythe declared, "All mainframe systems shut down nineteen seconds ago. Missile systems are frozen. Congratulations, Mr. Taine. You did it. With nearly one minute to spare."

-4-

Much later, Taine, Ms. Smythe, whose first name turned out to be Pamela, and General Parker celebrated saving the world with the best meal possible at the NAEDS Base. Which, considering the importance of the installation and some of its visitors, was spectacular. During the course of the meal, the detective described in detail his encounter with the computer.

"Amazing," said the general, when Taine finished speaking. "To think you were able to save the world by connecting the horror of AIDS to Nostradamus's prediction."

Taine chuckled. "Not really. It was the first thing that came to mind. If I hadn't thought of AIDS, I would have found something else that worked. Given enough time, I could have produced a dozen different meanings for the verse. My only problem was producing evidence quickly enough to convince the computer. That was the real challenge.

"Prophecy is a wonderful scam, General. It has nothing to do with actually predicting the future. The trick is to make a statement so vague, so non-specific, it could mean a hundred different things.

"Fortunetellers do it all the time. A gypsy tells her gullible client she will meet a tall, dark stranger in the near future. The seeress would never dare be more specific. *Near* could be next week, next month, even next year. Tall and dark are equally vague. The validity of the prediction relies entirely on the victim's perceptions. Sooner or later, she has to encounter someone matching the correct description. And remember with awe the gypsy soothsayer's words."

"But...Nostradamus..." began the general.

"...was only slightly more specific than my hypothetical gypsy woman," said Taine. "His predictions were worded in such a manner that any one of them could have a dozen different meanings. Before World War II, nearly a hundred of the quatrains were said to describe Napoleon's conquests. During and after the war, occultists claimed the same verses dealt with Hitler. Recently, a few enterprising souls connected the identical lines with Saddam Hussein."

The detective shook his head. "The game never ends."

Pamela Smythe leaned over and patted Taine on the hand. "True, but not true. Prophecy is a sham, but it does often come to pass. The predictions themselves can alter the future. Wetherby's actions, feeding the quatrains into the mainframe, prove it.

"Think of what would have happened if you hadn't been able to shut down the NAEDS computer. The missile attack would have been launched, bringing about an end of civilization, perhaps of all life on our planet. To me, that sounds like the Final Apocalypse. Which means that everything in the verse as you originally described it to us would have taken place. Exactly as the Frenchman stated."

Taine nodded. "You're right. I can almost hear Nostradamus laughing at us from the grave. Armageddon would have occurred, brought about by the very verse predicting it. It would have been the seer's most amazing triumph." Taine paused, as if awed by the notion. "Hundreds of years after his death, Nostradamus would have been responsible for the greatest self-fulfilling prophecy of all time."

Ms. Sydney Taine patrols not only alternate realities, but time itself. And she's not above borrowing a trick from her brother...

KISS ME DEADLY

-1-

"Y ou seen today's paper?" asked Ape Largo as he thrust the tightly rolled newspaper at Sydney Taine.

"No, not yet," replied his boss. Taine placed one hand over her mouth to suppress a yawn. With the other, she gracefully retrieved the newspaper from his grasp. Laying the tabloid in the middle of her cluttered desk, she tried to flatten it out. Ape Largo didn't just read a newspaper; he mutilated it. "I was out late last night. Slept till noon and had a quick lunch at the Waldorf. Didn't have a chance to talk to anyone about the news on the way here. I miss anything important?"

"Nah," said Largo. He shrugged his immense shoulders. Standing just a few inches over five feet, he was one of a handful of men who was as wide as he was tall. With thick black hair and features ugly enough to shatter most mirrors, Largo knew he looked more brute than human. That he worked as a detective – or any occupation requiring reasoning power – surprised most people. They usually assumed that human speech was well beyond his mental capabilities, an opinion he tried hard not to dispel. As an investigator, it helped immensely to have suspects think him thick as a brick.

"Nothing important. Just the front page headline screaming how the cops found 'Little Boy' Wilson's body last night down by the waterfront."

"Little Boy's dead…?"

"As the proverbial doornail. Need I mention that there wasn't a mark on his body? Not a bottle of bootleg booze anywhere in the area. Could have been a natural death, except for the fact his skin was crinkled and dry like yellowed parchment. If the police hadn't found his wallet in his coat pocket, they would never have guessed who it was. Take a gander at his picture. Little Boy looks like he's a few hundred years old."

Taine stared at the dead man's photo on the tabloid's front page. The owner of the *New York Daily Telegraph* believed in shock journalism. Dead men didn't tell tales, but they sold a lot of newspapers.

"Wilson's definitely seen better days," said Taine. The shrunken, shriveled features looked like those of a centuries-old mummy. Nothing at all like the six-foot-five mobster they had tangled with on more than one occasion in the past. "No wounds anywhere? You sure?"

"Read the paper." Largo plunked himself down on the overstuffed and somewhat battered yellow sofa at the rear of the office. The springs groaned under his weight. His body wasn't made for ordinary chairs. "Not a scratch. Just like the other two."

"Three major-league bootleggers dead in the past two weeks," said Taine. "All dead under very mysterious circumstances. Our esteemed police chief make a statement yet?"

"The usual," said Largo. "The cops are working hard on the case and expect an arrest any day. And I'm da tooth fairy."

"I never knew," said Taine with a smile. "The chief mention anything about Bruno King's death?"

"Nah. That would be admitting we got a gang war in our fair city. You know the chief would never say anything like that in public."

"Well, just over a month ago the police killed Bruno King

– the biggest, meanest bootlegger in the city – in a shootout at his warehouse," said Taine, drumming her fingers on the desktop. "Now, three of his rivals, each one anxious to take over King's territory, end up dead. Coincidence? I don't think so. I'd be willing to bet the murders are all connected."

"I never gamble," said Largo.

"Neither do I," said Taine. "Wasn't there talk about Bruno having a silent partner?"

"Yeah, but nothing very definite. King was plenty tough, but he wasn't smart. Lots of people, including me, assumed he had help setting up his bootlegging operation. Now we'll never know the truth."

"Never say never. Especially when it involves a case."

"We're investigating the murders?" asked Largo. "Since when?"

"Since noon today. Rocco 'The Block' called me late this morning. Both he and Terry Doyle are scared out of their minds. They're the ones who took me to lunch at the Waldorf. They know they're next on the list. They're willing to pay big money for us to find their would-be assassin."

"Gangsters paying us to catch other gangsters. Lovely. How do you know these clowns ain't the killers?"

"Neither man has the brains to pull off these crimes," said Taine, shuffling the papers on her desk, looking for something. "Rocco's a good man with a knife. Boyle's an Irish cowboy, packing two pistols under his coat. Our three corpses were stiff as a board and dried out like week-old bread. Not our clients' style, not at all."

"You got a theory?"

"Not yet, but I have some ideas." Taine snapped her fingers, then pulled open the top desk drawer and retrieved a small pill container. With a flick of the wrist, she popped the top open and dropped a small white tablet into her mouth.

"Aspirin?" asked Largo. "Got a hangover from cheap booze?"

"Nonsense," said Taine. "I never drink cheap stuff. These lozenges freshen my breath. I like the taste."

Tucking the pill bottle into the waist of her skirt, Taine rose from the chair. Tall and slender, she looked more like a silent film star than New York City's first female private detective. She stood five feet seven in her bare feet, weighed a shade over one hundred and twenty pounds, and liked to dress in a colorful long skirt and pleated white blouse. Unlike many of the newly liberated women of the times, Taine wore no jewelry and no makeup. With long black hair that fell almost to her waist and flashing black eyes, she needed none. Everybody who was anybody in Manhattan knew Sydney Taine.

Taine stared out the office windows at the streets of downtown Manhattan. The view from fifteen stories above the street was spectacular. The location cost money, but their business – Taine and Largo Investigations – made enough to pay for it and much, much more. Taine's society connections put the firm on the fast track, and their clients included many of Manhattan's movers and shakers. Both legal and illegal.

"Is it possible," said Taine, her voice echoing off the glass windows, "that Bruno King somehow survived his gun battle with the police?"

"I saw his body in the morgue," said Largo. "Not even Lon Chaney is *that* good. No one came forward to claim the corpse, so he was buried in an unmarked pauper's grave. I don't think most of his gang was sorry to see him dead. The guy was a kill-crazy lunatic."

"They might not have cared about his corpse, but someone wants control of the bootleg operation he left behind. It's our job to find out who, and do it before that person kills our two clients."

"Easier said than done," said Largo. "Where do we start?"

"Drive up to Harlem. I want you to go visit Father Leon. See if he knows anything about these murders."

"That fraud," said Largo, grimacing. "Living the high life while his parishioners struggle in poverty."

"He's a weasel," said Taine, "but he's not stupid. Father

Leon comes from Haiti. Show him Little Boy Wilson's picture and see if it reminds him of anything. Ask him about the dead who walk."

"You think some sort of black magic's involved in these deaths?" asked Largo. Taine was an expert in subjects most people considered unmentionable. And often unholy.

"Three people murdered without a mark on them, wrinkled and aged like they've been dead a hundred years? Yeah, that makes me think the dark arts might be involved."

"You're the boss," said Largo, bounding off the sofa and heading for the door. He turned his head for an instant and stared at Taine. "Do me a favor, though. Don't try anything foolish while I'm gone, okay? Stay here. Three men are dead already. Let's keep it right there. Don't forget – you're the brains of this outfit. I'm just the muscle. So no heroics."

"Don't worry," Taine said, then flipped another lozenge into her mouth, "I'll be careful."

It wasn't until Largo was driving uptown that he realized Sydney hadn't said a word about remaining in the office.

-2-

Father Leon stood six feet, three inches tall and weighed a little more than one hundred and thirty pounds. His dark, dark skin was the color of expensive Belgian chocolate. He had muted brown eyes and closely cropped grey hair. His face was clean-shaven, absolutely smooth. Though he was obviously elderly, no one knew exactly how old Father Leon was. Nor did he ever say.

Father Leon had lived in Harlem since the turn of the century. A gifted speaker and charismatic leader, he'd founded the First Church of African Identity in 1900, proclaiming that the new century would be one of opportunity and enlightenment for black men and women. His religious message – one of duty to church, community, and country – was popular with both the white establishment and the poor people of Harlem. As his church prospered, so did Father Leon.

He made it quite clear to anyone who listened that he believed that the poor and downtrodden learned best by example. And he set an example of success few could equal.

Father Leon lived in a mansion slightly less elaborate than the mayor's residence, complete with servants, bodyguards, and a private chef. Father Leon claimed his extravagant ways provided positive motivation to his parishioners. The preacher claimed to be a man of the people, a common priest who had worked hard for his wealth. Largo was one of the very few who felt otherwise.

Ape didn't like Father Leon. He considered the priest little more than a blood-sucking parasite living off the poor. There were nearly one thousand members of the First Church of African Identity, a vast majority living in substandard apartments in some of the city's worst neighborhoods. They needed food and jobs and better living conditions, not examples.

Still, Sydney had sent him to talk to Father Leon, and Ape did what his boss told him to do. That didn't mean he had to like it. Largo liked it even less when he was forced to wait. And wait.

On Thursdays Father Leon held his weekly meeting with the mayor, police chief, and city services manager. The meetings were little more than courtesy calls, but the politicians felt they sent a positive message to the city's working poor. They made it appear that the city cared for them as much as it did for the rich and powerful; from garbage pickup to ambulance service to police patrols, no neighborhood was treated differently than any other. Or so they said. And Father Leon was always there, to assure his followers that everything the heads of the city said was true.

Darkness had descended upon Manhattan before Largo was finally escorted into the priest's fancy office. And only then, when they were alone, did Largo show him the picture of Little Boy Wilson he'd cut from the morning paper.

"This is bad," muttered Father Leon. "This is very bad."

The old man peered up from the photo, his brown eyes

flickering in the electric lights. "You say this man is the third to die in this manner? And that the famous lady detective, Sydney Taine, is investigating the case?"

"Yes, sir," said Largo, his hands folded neatly on the table in front of him. Being around any priest always made him feel like he was in fourth grade and, much as Ape hated to admit it, Father Leon had presence, an aura of absolute authority. "Two others were found in the past few weeks, in the exact same condition as Little Boy."

"Three will not be the end. There will be a fourth. And then a fifth. Tell Miss Taine that there will be more deaths. The undead walk by night."

"I'm not sure what you mean by that, Father," said Largo, "but I have a terrible feeling it's not good."

"In Haiti many years ago, I saw a *houngan* – a magic man – make the dead walk," said Father Leon softly, his eyes burning with mysterious fire. "Using the power of the Loas, the gods of Vodun, he could animate a corpse and have it perform simple tasks, like help with the harvest and load wagons for market. Such creatures – *zombies* – are harmless. Their minds are empty of all malice. They are not to be feared."

"Uh huh," said Largo noncommittally. Working for the past three years with Sydney Taine had taught him that real magic existed. And, despite Father Leon's comments to the contrary, it was almost always something to be feared. "Where's this leading, Father?"

"I was told there was another path." The priest's voice was barely a whisper. "The Left-Hand Way, practiced only by *bokors* – traveling magicians – who would do anything for a price. This ritual was called *Le Baiser de L'Homme Mort*, the Kiss of the Dead Man. Using a spell so foul it could not be uttered aloud, the *bokor* served as a gateway for those whose evil survived beyond death. Those who wished to return."

"A dead man who wanted to be brought back to life?"

"Exactly," said the priest. "Using dark magic, a *bokor* can reunite an evil spirit with its original body. But such a being is much more than a mere zombie. It possesses the strengths of both the living and the dead. Ordinary weapons – bullets or knives – cannot harm it. Nor will fire burn it.

"This monster," continued Father Leon, his voice shaking, "exists in a state of constant hunger. It requires the life-energies of mortals to remain strong. It feeds on living souls to maintain its unnatural life. The Vodun priests called this horror, this abomination, the thirsty dead."

"Then maybe it's not Bruno King's rivals who are trying to take over his territory," Largo muttered as he pondered all that the priest had said. "Maybe one of these *bokor* character brought Bruno's body and soul back together…"

"That may be the truth," said Father Leon. "And the resurrected dead man will devour the soul of anyone who stands in his way. Including yours, Mr. Largo, and that of Miss Sydney Taine."

-3-

Traffic in Manhattan was snarled and it took Largo nearly an hour to return to the office. Every night, the city stepped closer and closer to complete gridlock. City planners predicted that by 1930, traffic would be so bad in Manhattan that cabs would be banned from the streets. Largo wasn't sure if he liked that idea, but tonight he would have voted for it without hesitation. Getting anywhere in the city at dinnertime was a nightmare. By the time he reached their office building, he was dripping sweat. Needless to say, the elevator was out and he had to scramble up fifteen flights of stairs to their floor. The few late-departing office workers who spotted him swore a gorilla had escaped from the city zoo and was loose in the building. With so much bad gin being passed around in speakeasies, the police heard their complaints and dismissed them.

Reaching the office door, Largo banged his huge right fist hard onto the baked blue glass. *Thud, thud, thud!* There was enough power in those blows to stir the dust and send the stale air in the quiet corridor swirling into unexpected motion. *Thud, thud, thud!* This time accompanied by a semi-human howl: "Sydney, if you're inside, open the damned door! Open it now, or I'm breaking it down!"

"Hey, Ugly," came a voice from the rear of the hall. That was all Largo needed to hear to recognize the speaker. Only one hoodlum was foolish enough to mock him: Elton Porter, a lowlife street thug and member of Bruno King's old gang. "She's not there."

"Yeah," said Largo, turning. "How do you know, Elton? And where is she?"

Elton was a short, stocky man dressed in braided trousers, a yellow shirt that looked as if it had been put together by weaving short pieces of twisted yarn, and dark brown twine sandals. He liked to pretend he was a dangerous outlaw from down South, but Largo knew that Elton was a born and raised in NYC. "Left an hour ago, did Miss Taine. But she told me to wait for you here."

"How nice," said Largo, his fingers curling and uncurling into fists. "Sydney left for parts unknown, but she left you to tell me she's gone. Why do I suspect this isn't quite the whole story?"

"Hey, pal," said Porter, raising both hands as if in surrender, "take it easy. I didn't do nothing wrong. You remember my brother Ralph? He's the one escorting Miss Taine to the ceremony tonight out on the Island. Nothing wrong about that. Your boss wanted information, and we provided it for the right price.

"When she left, Miss Taine told me to stick around for the Big Ugly…" he raised his hands again "…her words, pal, not mine – and to make sure you have directions. She said you'd tear the building apart piece by piece, making a big fuss, if I wasn't here to tell you what's what."

"Sydney's gone to Long Island?" rumbled Largo. "With your brother Ralph, who I hear is even shorter on brains than you? To witness some sort of voodoo ceremony, I assume. Why didn't she leave a message for me in the office? That's what she usually does when she goes someplace like this."

"Simple explanation," said Elton Porter, taking a step closer to Largo, then another. A disarming grin spread across the man's face. He held out his right hand, his fingers wrapped around a small object. "Miss Taine left this with me to give to you. It explains everything."

Porter was only a few feet away from Largo. Still grinning, he raised his closed fist up to Largo's face.

"Hey, watch what you're doing!" said Largo, momentarily caught off guard.

"Here's the answers," said Porter, uncurling his fingers. A small shape in the center of his palm burst with a loud snap. A thin strand of smoke rose like a snake from Porter's hand and into Largo's startled face.

"What the...?" began Largo, but he never finished the sentence. The odor of dead flowers filled his nostrils and he collapsed to the floor, unconscious.

-4.-

Largo awoke with a killer headache. He was face-down in what seemed to be the trunk of a roadster. His hands were pulled behind his back, his wrists held together by handcuffs. A yellow drop cloth covered his body. The air was foul but breathable. A steady rocking motion told Largo the car was on the highway. Most likely on the way to the ceremony Elton had mentioned. Largo felt like a total idiot, letting himself be hijacked so easily. But, there was nothing he could do about it now. Whatever disaster awaited him at the trip's end, worrying about it wasn't going to do any good. Instead, Largo closed his eyes and pondered exactly what he'd do to Elton once he got his hands on him.

The auto came to a stop twenty minutes later. Wherever they were going, they had arrived. Largo tested the steel binding his wrists. He was strong, stronger than anyone he had ever met, but pulling handcuffs apart wasn't possible. Still, his legs were free, and when the time came, he could do plenty of damage with them.

Another five minutes passed before Largo heard muffled voices through the closed trunk. "He's not so tough, if you ask me," Elton Porter said. "Big muscles but a small, small brain."

"Enough of your mouthing off," said the other man, whose voice Largo didn't recognize. "Ceremony's gonna start in just a few minutes. We gotta be there."

The trunk opened abruptly. Rough hands pulled the yellow drop cloth off Largo's body and yanked him from his makeshift prison so swiftly that he didn't have time to fight. It took his eyes a few seconds to adjust to the moonlight. By then, he was out of the trunk and standing, albeit somewhat shakily. Elton Porter stood at Largo's side, holding him by his right elbow, while a man who looked enough like the hoodlum to be his double did the same on the left.

"Ralph Porter, right?" asked Largo, stalling for a little time. The car, a bright yellow Oldsmobile coupe, was parked with six or seven others in a small dirt lot in the rear of what appeared to be an old mansion. The place was indistinguishable from a hundred other similar houses on Long Island, save for the weird yellow light flickering from its large barn. Largo could hear men's voices, though he couldn't make out what was being said. Evidently they were the last to arrive. "Where's my boss? If you hurt her, you're going to regret it for the rest of your very short life."

"Big talk," said Ralph with a laugh. "I didn't do nothing to the lady. Didn't have to. See, she's got a date with someone real important. First date, first kiss." Ralph laughed again. It was high-pitched and annoying. "First and last kiss."

"Now look who's talking too much," said Elton. He dragged Largo forward by the arm. "The boss is waiting for us. Let's go."

Largo went. He could have resisted, could have made it impossible for the two men to drag him anywhere, but he didn't. The Porter brothers were cheap thugs with a taste for brutality. Yet neither of them had laid a hand on him. Not one punch, not one kick, not even the usual eye gouge or kick to the groin. They were treating him with kid gloves. It didn't make sense. At least, not yet.

The situation only got more outrageous when they reached the barn. Just before the three of them entered, Ralph Porter reached behind Largo, fumbled with the handcuffs for a second, and then they were gone. At the same instant, Elton Porter retrieved a sawed-off shotgun from beside the door and pressed the barrel into Largo's side. "Try anything, Big Ugly," he declared, "and I'll splatter your insides all over the floor."

"You're here to learn a lesson," said Ralph, shoving an automatic into the small of Largo's back. "Watch and listen and don't make any sudden moves. Afterward, we drive you back to the city and let you go to tell everyone what you saw. Try something stupid, and we'll find ourselves another witness. Understand?"

"Yeah, I understand," said Largo.

The wooden barn's interior was poorly lit by a pair of gas lanterns. Along with a majority of Bruno King's old gang, Largo also recognized three crooked cops and at least one of the mayor's aides. The two dozen or so lowlifes were all standing, waiting. Some looked curious, others looked concerned, and still others frightened. None of them seemed happy to be there.

The reason for their discomfort was quite obvious. In the center of the barn was a large platform. Almost like a stage, it stood two feet high, about ten feet long, and six feet wide. At the platform's far edge, propped up like a wood monolith, rested a large coffin. Black soil and dark green cemetery mold clung to its side and top. The box appeared battered and bruised, no doubt the result of the casket being lowered and later raised from the earth.

Largo didn't have much time to stare. A hulking gangster rolled a man in a wheelchair up a ramp onto the wood platform. The man in the chair wore a black slouch hat and a heavy black overcoat with the collar raised. A black scarf was wrapped around his neck, so that his features were completely hidden. Largo had no idea who the man could be, other than it wasn't Sydney Taine. Taine wouldn't be caught dead in black.

"Bring out the woman," commanded the wheelchair-bound man. His voice was so muffled by his scarf that it was hard to hear what he was saying. "Let the ceremony begin."

"Don't even twitch," growled Elton Porter, "or it'll be the last move you ever make."

From the opposite end of the barn, two hoodlums slouched forward. Walking between them, with the faint twist of a smile on her face, was Sydney Taine. There were no ropes or chains on her arms or legs, but it was clear that she was a prisoner. Still, Taine didn't seem the slightest bit concerned. With her usual swagger, she marched up the three steps leading to the stage. Her escorts, surprised by her lack of fear, followed her onto the platform.

Largo said nothing. Neither did he move. Taine never gambled. She had emphasized that point earlier in the day. Still, Largo's faith in his boss didn't stop a trickle of cold sweat from dripping down his back.

The man in the wheelchair was less impressed. His body shook with unheard laughter. "Open the coffin," he commanded.

One of the two thugs accompanying Taine did exactly that. The lid came off easily. It had been removed before. A babble of shocked voices greeted what was inside. Even Largo cursed in dismay.

The thirsty dead, Father Leon had called them. If anything, the name minimized the horror of the thing inside the coffin: the desiccated, decaying corpse of Bruno King. And while it wasn't alive, neither was it dead.

King had been a big man with thick neck, heavy jowls, and jutting chin. No longer. Death had drawn the fat and muscle from his body; his skin stretched across his bones like old shoe leather. Fingers once the size of sausages had shrunk into claws and the cheap suit in which he'd been interred hung off his frame like a sheet on a broom handle. His skull still bore the marks of the three bullets that had ended his life; the bones hung together by thin brown threads of rotting flesh. His nose was completely gone. His lips were drawn back in a permanent snarl, revealing a mouth filled with yellowed teeth. His eyes had disappeared, food for worms. But in their sockets burned a blood-red fire. The fire of unholy life.

"Bruno King died," said the wheelchair-bound man. "He has returned. His will is stronger than Death itself. He offers each of you a choice – serve him or die. Three of your number refused. All three are dead. Now, tonight, another fool, an outsider, questions his authority. She, too, must pay the price."

"Long live Bruno King," yelled Elton from his position by Largo. "Long live the king of Manhattan!"

As if responding to the words, Bruno King stepped from his coffin. Slowly, but steadily, he shuffled forward in a ghastly parody of life. The crowd surrounding the stage melted back, muttering their innermost fears aloud. Eyes shining like fire, the zombie approached Sydney Taine.

Muscles tensed in Largo's arms and shoulders. "One step," whispered Ralph Porter, pushing the pistol deeper into Ape's back, "and I'll squeeze the trigger."

The zombie raised its arms. Its bone-white fingers clutched the air. King's lips cracked apart, his yellow teeth gleaming in the moonlight.

"Now suffer the Kiss of the Dead Man, Sydney Taine," said the wheelchair man. "And die."

Up to that moment, it seemed to Largo that every word, every event of the evening had been carefully planned. Some unknown, unseen playwright had set the scene, placed the props. The only problem was, no one had given Sydney Taine a script. And she, whether acting the detective or the adventurer, loved to improvise.

Taine raised one hand and flipped two white tablets into her mouth. Then, to the amazement of every person in the room – including Ape Largo – she stepped forward eagerly.

She walked right into the zombie's outstretched arms and declared loud enough for everyone present to hear, "Hey, honey. Kiss me deadly."

Her long, slender fingers circling the dead man's fragile skull, Taine pulled Bruno King's rotting face to hers and kissed him full on the lips.

A shudder of revulsion swept through the crowd. Grown men turned green and at least one onlooker lost his dinner.

The kiss ended, and Taine, looking no worse for the gruesome encounter, slid back from between the zombie's arms. Smiling, she looked around at her two captors. "What about it, guys?" Largo heard her say, "How about a kiss?"

The question still hung in the air when the zombie's eyes flared an intense crimson. A grotesque sound throbbed in the barn, the sound of a dead man desperately trying to scream with lungs that had been devoid of air for months. The monster spun around, turning to the safety of its coffin, but time had run out.

Bruno King's head exploded like a Halloween pumpkin with a firecracker inside. Splashes of rotted flesh and chipped bone spattered the audience. The headless corpse lurched one, two, three steps forward, then collapsed in a heap on the stage.

For an instant, no one moved or said a word. Then, an overwhelming dread swept through the crowd and two dozen screaming, howling, cursing men scrambled for the exit.

"Come back!" screamed the man in the wheelchair, but no one listened.

Largo made good use of the chaos. He swung about, catching Ralph square in the chest with an elbow. Grabbing Ralph's pistol, Largo slammed it into Elton's forehead. A kick to the groin sent the second Porter boy to the floor, the shotgun slipping from his suddenly nerveless fingers. A quick tap to the head with the pistol barrel sent Ralph tumbling on top of his brother. The skirmish was over in less than thirty seconds.

Largo turned toward the stage, concerned about his boss's

safety. He need not have worried. Only two people remained on the platform: Sydney Taine and the man in the wheelchair. Though Largo had serious doubts about how helpless the invalid really was. His suspicions were confirmed an instant later as the man rose from the wheelchair, obviously deciding that a quick exit was required.

"You're not going anywhere," said Sydney Taine. The small, but deadly derringer she held pointed at the mystery man's chest gave suitable weight to her words. Largo never could figure out where Taine kept her gun and he was too much the gentleman to ask. "All the voodoo in the world won't stop a bullet through your heart."

Largo was on the platform now, at Taine's side. He whipped the hat and scarf from the mystery man, revealing the scowling visage of Father Leon. "Why am I not surprised?" Ape said.

"I admit nothing," said Father Leon. He settled back into the wheelchair as if it were a throne. "Call the police. And my lawyer."

Taine hooked an arm in Largo's and led him a little ways off. "You knew?" she asked, daintily stepping over the headless body of Bruno King. "When did you guess?"

"Pretty early," said Largo. "We just take the case at lunchtime and you're kidnapped in the middle of the afternoon. The only ones who know about our investigation are Father Leon and our clients. Seemed pretty stupid for the guys paying the bills to make the snatch.

"Then, two thugs escort me to a voodoo ceremony to watch you get killed. They sure wanted to convince me a zombie was taking over the bootleg business. I'm sure they had orders to let me escape once the ceremony ended, allowing me to warn any potential rivals what a terrible mistake it would be to go up against the undead Mr. King. Who really benefits? The guy who knows all about zombies. That had to be Father Leon."

Taine nodded. "Bruno kept the gang in line, but Father Leon was the brains behind the bootleg business all along.

Secretly he'd been in charge of the gang for years. Didn't matter how much money he took in from his church, he wanted more. When the police killed King, it looked like the end of the money train for Leon. Until he came up with the zombie angle. He'd be puppet master again, only he'd use a dead man instead of a live one as his front."

"Not a bad idea," said Largo, one eye still trained on Father Leon. There was no way the elderly priest was going anywhere. "Especially when he could back it up with the real goods. I gather that the voodoo ceremony was no fake? Ditto the Kiss of the Dead Man?"

"The ceremony was real," said Taine. "Same for the kiss. Father Leon learned them both long ago, when he lived in Haiti. Dangerous stuff. The zombie required the life-force of humans to stay animate. It killed those three men and would have killed me too, if I hadn't been prepared."

"Your throat lozenges?" said Largo.

"Salt tablets," said Taine. "After Rocco the Block hired me, I decided they might be useful. Zombies are creatures of corruption and decay. Salt's mankind's first and most powerful preservative, the ultimate enemy of decay. One taste of salt and Bruno was finished."

"Very effective," said Largo. "And dramatic. Leaving me with only one question. What do we do with him?" He nodded toward Father Leon. "Cops might want some hard evidence and we don't have much to offer."

"You're right. We've got nothing that'll stand up in court," said Taine. "He didn't kill anyone, the zombie did. And from what I can tell, his ties with Bruno's mob are very well hidden. It'd be our word against his – and that of his friends in City Hall."

"So?"

"So, I've decided to let him go free."

"Free?" said Largo.

"As a bird," said Taine, smiling. She turned to the priest. "Father Leon, you're free to leave. Though, I believe our clients want to have a word with you first. Something about the plans you had for prematurely ending their careers..."

Rocco the Block and Terry Doyle stepped out of the shadows. All the blood drained from Father Leon's features. Once more taking her partner by the arm, Sydney headed for the barn door. As she passed Terry Doyle, the gangster nodded and handed her a check.

"Case closed," said Sydney Taine. And it was.

THE CHILDREN OF MAY

-1-

"I will pay you one million dollars," said the man with the coal-black eyes, "if you will take this case, Mr. Taine."

Sidney Taine, known in Chicago and less reputable locations as "The New Age Detective," blinked in astonishment. He had been offered large fees before, but never one of this magnitude. Most men in his field would do just about anything for a million dollars. But his integrity was not for sale.

Folding his fingers together, Taine shook his head. "I never accept an assignment without first knowing the details involved, no matter what the price."

"You don't need the money?" asked the other man, sounding surprised.

Sitting erect in the yellow chair, facing Taine across a wide desk, the speaker looked like a military man at full attention. Only a touch of grey at his temples and the lines around his dark eyes betrayed the fact that he was nearly seventy years old. Wilson Kramer was one of the richest men in America. On the board of a dozen corporations and owner of one of the largest shipping firms in the world, he was the confidant of presidents, premiers, and kings. Why a man of his wealth and influence needed the help of Sidney Taine was a mystery. The answer to which, Taine felt sure, would soon be revealed.

"I didn't say that. I just want it clear from the beginning that my principles aren't for sale."

"So I've been told," said Kramer, with the slightest hint of a smile. "The same sources say you're the best detective there is at finding things. Especially things that most people think only exist in legends. There is talk of the Holy Grail and certain nails, among other items."

"I refuse to disbelieve, which often is half the solution."

"Do you believe in *Excalibur*? I will pay you one million dollars if you discover the hiding place of King Arthur's mythical sword."

The detective sighed. Lately, his career seemed to consist of taking on one impossible case after another. He wondered if his reputation was becoming more a hindrance than a help. So much publicity, he decided, made life extremely difficult.

Taine rose from his chair. He walked over to the huge picture window in his office and looked out on Lake Michigan. Whenever troubled, the detective stared at the great lake. Its placid waters calmed his nerves.

Taine said, "According to Mallory, Arthur gave Excalibur to Sir Bedevere to throw into a lake."

"Three times," said Kramer, surprising the detective with his knowledge of the legend. Then, remembering the millionaire's reputation for thoroughness, Taine realized it wasn't surprising at all. "Bedevere didn't want to do it and tried to hide the sword, but Arthur finally forced the knight to obey him."

"And when Sir Bedevere flung it into the water, a hand caught it, shook and brandished it three times, then disappeared into the lake," said Taine. "That was the last time the sword was ever seen. Recovering it might not be possible."

"I'm willing to take that chance. Occult scholars claim that Elaine, the Lady of the Lake, retrieved the blade, as well as the scabbard in which it was sheathed. According to tradition, she keeps them safe for the day Arthur returns from Avalon."

"A thousand years have passed since those events took place, if they ever actually occurred. You could be wasting your money."

"Let me worry about that. I'm convinced that if Excalibur can be found, you're the one to do it."

Taine grimaced. "And if my search proves fruitless?"

"I'll pay you half the fee merely for trying." There was a quiet desperation in the millionaire's voice, not apparent until now. "You're my last hope. If you fail, then I'm finished."

"Finished? Maybe you'd better explain."

"That need not concern you," said Kramer, his voice suddenly harsh. "Suffice it to say, my reasons are perfectly legal and in no way harmful to any person, living or dead. For now, consider it the whim of an old and very wealthy fool. If you learn of the blade's location, you'll know the rest."

Taine nodded. "Very well, I accept the assignment."

"Remember, I need the sword. Find it. Quickly. We don't have much time left."

Taine did not ask to whom 'we' referred.

-2-

A week later, Taine was ready for desperate measures. He had spent long hours poring through rare and forgotten books of occult lore, searching for some reference to either Excalibur or the mysterious Lady of the Lake, without finding a clue. Every day, Wilson Kramer called, checking on his progress. And every day, Taine was forced to admit the same results. Nothing.

Even his contacts, usually reliable in matters both mundane and occult, came up short. Taine belonged to a half-dozen secret societies. Their membership included those who moved in the fringe between the normal and supernormal worlds. Powerful beings, whose existence went unsuspected by humanity, they possessed knowledge beyond human ken. But none of them knew the fate of Excalibur.

"I'll be out of town for the rest of the week," Taine told

Mrs. McConnell, his secretary and sometime assistant. With business booming, and the daily calls from Kramer, he'd needed to bring her in once more. "You should be able to handle anything that comes up. If any major problems arise, contact Paul Schultz and let his agency deal with them. When Mr. Kramer calls, tell him I'm working on his case, and I'll contact him as soon as I have news."

"What are you planning? Nothing dangerous, I hope."

"I know how to take care of myself."

"I always worry when you insist on playing with forces best left alone," she said as Taine headed for the door. "Be careful."

He arrived at his destination shortly before sunset. The house was located in Chicago's far west suburbs, a solitary structure built at the intersection of three roads. According to ancient myths, such crossroads were sacred to Hecate, goddess of witchcraft. It was one of several properties Taine owned. Certain, very specific, locations were necessary for the performance of arcane rites. It was here, in a room curtained and painted entirely in black, that the detective intended to summon a demon from the outermost night. An extremely risky procedure, Taine saw it as his only hope in discovering Excalibur's location. If a demon couldn't tell him where the sword rested, then the blade was lost beyond all hope of recovery.

Three days he spent purifying his body and his spirit. During that time, he meditated, ate no meat, and drank only water. He walked barefoot, wearing only a robe of white cotton. Much of the time he spent concentrating on the infinite powers of good that existed in the universe, in a unity that bound together all living creatures. Taine purged all thoughts of failure from his mind. Success depended on an absolute faith in himself.

On the evening of the third day, Taine showered and changed into his magician's robes. Made of white linen, the outfit covered his entire body. On his feet he wore white slippers and on his head, a four-sided white cap on which was inscribed the four major names of power.

At the center of the floor of the black room, Taine drew his magic circle in white chalk. He followed traditions thousands of years old. The magical barrier consisted of an outer circle, nine feet in diameter, with an inner circle, a foot less in diameter, inscribed within the first. Between the two, Taine wrote in Latin the words "The Lord My Shepherd," to serve as a barrier against the thing he planned on summoning.

A brazier filled with oil went in the center of the figure. Next to it, Taine laid a silk cloth bundle containing a sword, knife, magic wand, and wax candle. After making a final check of the black room for anything out of order, the detective entered the circle through a small gap left unfinished in the two rings. Once inside, he used his chalk to complete the figures.

Taine carefully examined the circles. The smallest break in the lines would be fatal. A few extra minutes wasted seemed a small price to pay when risking both his body and soul. Finally satisfied, the detective inscribed the double seal of Solomon, the hexagram, inside the circles. He lit the brazier of oil to begin the ceremony.

Raising the sacrificial knife, Taine cut his left arm and let three drops of blood fall into the fire. Magic required blood, and three drops symbolized the Trinity. Laying the blade on the floor, Taine lifted the hazel wand and started chanting the evocation.

"I conjure thee, Ashtaroth, revealer of secrets of the past, by the power of Almighty God; by him that spake and it was done; by the Most Holy Names Adonai, El, Elohim, and Tetragrammaton."

The spell came from *The Lemegeton, The Lesser Key of Solomon*, one of the most powerful books of magic ever written. Few magicians understood or controlled the secrets contained in its pages. Taine was one of those few.

It took ten minutes to complete the summoning. His voice loud and clear, Taine finished the spell by proclaiming, "By the dreaded Day of Judgment, by the Seven Seals, by the Fire Before the Throne, and the Mighty Wisdom of God, I command you to appear." With a whisper of sound and a swirl of dark smoke that filled the entire chamber, the demon Ashtaroth was there.

He stood inches outside the circle, peering inward. Dressed in a loose-fitting red tunic, his skin glowing golden with good health, his blue eyes clear as crystal, he resembled an innocent little boy no more than seven or eight years old. "Who are you?" the demon asked, in the sweet voice of a child. "What do you want of me?"

"Information," said Taine. "Answer my questions, and I will set you free."

The golden child smiled. "I love questions. Let me step a little closer, and I will answer any question you might ask. The secrets of the universe will be yours."

Taine grinned without humor and gripped the hilt of his sword. He pointed the tip of the blade at the demon. "Not tonight, demon. You cannot pass through the circle. By the Sword and the Seals, I command you to obey my wishes."

The child that was Ashtaroth pouted. "Light the candle, annoying mortal. I will answer your queries until the wax burns down. No longer."

Taine nodded; he expected no more. He lit the candle using the flame from the brazier. "I am searching for Excalibur, the sword of King Arthur. Does it still exist?"

"I know of no sword by that name."

Taine drew in a deep breath, then slowly exhaled. The spell forced the demon to speak only truth, but truth was not always enough. According to some scholars, Excalibur was not the original name of Arthur's sword. It took a few precious seconds, watching the wax candle melt, before Taine remembered what he needed.

"I search for the sword, Caliburn. Does it exist?"

"It exists," answered the demon.

"Where is it?" Taine was aware the candle was burning much faster than normal. Another of the demon's tricks. But there was nothing he could do to stop it. The bargain was made.

"In England," said Ashtaroth. Then to the detective's surprise, the creature added, "At a school. I know not its name."

"At a school?"

Taine hesitated, puzzled by the demon's answer. Only the child's smirk of satisfaction made him realize he was wasting precious time. Which obviously was the reason Ashtaroth had volunteered the information.

"Who owns the sword?" Taine shouted, as the candle wick sputtered, the flame about to go out. "Who owns it?"

With a rush of wind and swirl of smoke Ashtaroth disappeared. Drifting through the emptiness came the demon's answer to the final question. "The Children of May. The blade is owned by The Children of May."

-3-

The next week proved even more frustrating than the one before. Taine had a name but nothing else. He didn't know if The Children of May referred to an organization, a religion, a cult, or perhaps even the offspring of a woman named May. And as before, all of his contacts proved equally ineffective in providing an answer.

Late in the afternoon, twenty days after he'd accepted Mr. Kramer's assignment, the detective sat behind his desk, eyes focused blearily on an ancient tome. Written in Latin, it was an extremely rare history of cults flourishing in the seventeenth century. He had borrowed it from a well-known antiquities collector through a combination of bribes, threats, and promises of future compensation. Unfortunately, so far as he'd read, the volume contained no mention of The Children of May.

Knocking first, Mrs. McConnell walked into Taine's office. "A Miss Lawrence is outside. I'd have handled her myself, but I thought you could use a nice break."

"Lawrence? Do I know her?"

"I don't think you've met. She's asking for donations to

the Chicago Battered Children's Shelter."

Taine frowned. When he looked down at the tome on his desk, the letters blurred. And something about this woman's arrival felt strange. He carefully shut the book and sighed. "Show her in. If I read another word about secret societies and mysterious orders, I'll go nuts. A few minutes in the real world might do me some good. Even if it means talking to an elderly maiden aunt."

Mrs. McConnell grinned at the detective's startled expression as she escorted the tall, slender blond into the office.

"I'm pleased to meet you, Mr. Taine," said Miss Lawrence, smiling as she shook hands with the detective. "Sorry if I disappointed you."

"Disappointed me? How?"

"I gather you were expecting someone older – and uglier."

Taine flushed, feeling very much the fool. "My apologies. Sometimes I have a big mouth."

Mrs. McConnell slipped out of the room as Miss Lawrence laughed. "Everyone expects people working for volunteer organizations to be old and grey. There are men and women of all ages working to help abused children, but there are never enough."

Taine nodded. "I admire your work. As a private detective, I deal with the underside of society. But most of the sordid details involve adults who bring their troubles on themselves. Dealing with innocent children would be too much for me."

For a moment, the innocent guise of Ashtaroth came to Taine. He shut it out of his mind.

Miss Lawrence had launched into her sales pitch, seeking a donation Taine had already decided to make. "...only the tip of the iceberg. Tens of thousands of children are beaten and abused each year by their parents. Some die. Others survive but are permanently scarred, either physically or mentally. A significant percentage run away, escaping one nightmare world only to enter another."

Taine nodded. Something strange in the cadence of Miss Lawrence's voice bothered him. He couldn't think well.

"Your donation," said Miss Lawrence, her eyes glistening with emotion, "would mean a great deal to the shelter. The money will help children who might not otherwise survive. Rescuing them from the cold, cruel sea into which they've been cast by uncaring parents," she said, and now Taine could feel his skin prickling, "figuratively speaking."

A chill swept through Taine. His huge hands gripped the edge of his desk, as if to steady himself. All blood drained from his face.

"Is something the matter?" asked Miss Lawrence. "Did I say something wrong?"

"The sea," muttered Taine, his mind racing. "He set them adrift in a boat in the harsh sea. The children of the lords and ladies, born on May Day. Merlin warned him, so he tried to kill them all. He tried but failed."

"Are you all right?"

"I'm fine," said Taine. He drew in a deep breath, then another, forcing his system to relax. Pieces of the puzzle began to fit together in his mind.

Then, rising out of his subconscious, another thought struck him. "Your organization must network with child abuse groups throughout the country, maybe the world. Do you recall ever dealing with a group in England called The Children of May?"

Miss Lawrence faltered for a moment before she answered. "The Children of May are well known in our field. They specialize in helping disadvantaged children abandoned by their families. They've been operating in Britain for years and years."

"For longer than you might imagine," said Taine.

-4-

Late that same evening, Taine met Wilson Kramer at the airport. The millionaire stood waiting outside his private jet, staring at his watch. Next to him, almost invisible in the darkness, was a little girl. Clutching Kramer's coat with one hand, she stared at Taine's face with wide eyes. Her other arm was wrapped possessively around a Cinderella doll.

Taine smiled at the child but remained quiet. After a few seconds, Wilson Kramer said, "This is my granddaughter, Penelope. She likes being called Penny." Almost defensively, he added, "She's coming with us."

"I'm very pleased to meet you, Penny," said Taine, bending over and offering his hand. After a second, the girl reached out and shook. Though the child looked perfectly healthy, Taine knew that not all wounds showed on the surface.

"What a nice doll. Does he have a name?"

"She's Cinderella," said Penny, laughing. "She's a girl."

"Oops," said Taine, acting surprised. "My mistake."

"I like you," said Penny. "You're silly."

"Penny," said Kramer, gently, "Go tell Mr. Johnson to prepare the plane for takeoff. Mr. Taine and I will board in a minute. Maybe if you're good, he'll let you stay in the cockpit."

"Okay, Grandpa. Let's go, 'Ella."

Once Penny was out of sight, Kramer turned to Taine. The millionaire's face was a cold, unreadable mask. But his voice trembled with emotion when he spoke. "Penny's my only grandchild. My daughter and her husband are dead. Killed in a car crash."

"I know," said Taine, wanting to spare the old man further heartbreak. "I read the story in the newspapers."

Kramer continued, as if not hearing Taine's words. "She was the only survivor. The only one who lived. But she needed blood. No one realized at the time it was tainted. Penny's the only one I have left. And she has AIDS."

The suddenly very, very old man stared into Taine's eyes. "Now do you understand why I have to find Excalibur? Why I was willing to spend my entire fortune to locate the magic sword?"

"Yes, I do."

Nodding, the millionaire turned and, without another word, entered the jet. Taine followed.

They landed in London in early morning. As they cleared customs, a tall, middle-aged man, bald except for a tiny fringe of hair above each ear, approached.

"Mr. Kramer? Mr. Taine?" he asked politely. "I'm Gerald Newton. I was sent here to meet you. My car is waiting outside."

"Sent?" asked Kramer suspiciously. "By whom?"

Penny, not the least bit concerned, smiled at the tall man. He winked at her and said, "By the people you want to see. By The Children of May."

Seeing the sudden look of concern that flashed between Taine and Kramer, Newton held up his hands in mock dismay. "Nothing mysterious about it, gentlemen. Miss Lawrence called hours ago about your trip." Newton smiled gently. "She is one of us. You must have known."

"I guessed as much," said Taine. "She was sent to check me out, wasn't she?"

Newton smiled slightly and tipped an imaginary hat. "I assure you we mean no harm. Violence is against all of our principles. Won't you please accompany me? It's a long ride. The sooner we leave, the sooner we arrive."

"I came to find a sword," said Kramer, his tone slow and measured. "A very famous sword. Do you have it?"

"Yes," said Newton, a note of sorrow creeping into his voice. "We have it. As well as the scabbard. Now, will you come?"

"Yes," answered Taine. "We will."

It was a long drive. They were several hundred miles outside of London, Taine estimated, before they finally reached their destination. He wasn't sure what he expected, but a huge idyllic estate, set up much like a college, with ivy-covered buildings amidst ancient, majestic trees and wide green lawns, caught him by surprise. As did the number of children who were there.

There were hundreds of them playing outside. Almost a thousand, he guessed. There were adults, too, supervising the games. Taine had never seen so many happy, carefree children in one place. All was peaceful, serene.

The sound of their laughter followed as Newton steered their car up a winding road to a solitary building far back from the path. It appeared to be a small chapel. There was no mistaking its great age.

Newton parked the car in a spot only a few feet from the building's main entrance. They all got out and stretched. After the long ride, it felt good to stand up.

"Perhaps Mistress Penny would like to engage in some activities with the other children?" said Newton, addressing his question directly to the young girl. "I believe a group of ladies her age serve their dollies tea each afternoon around this time. They would welcome a visitor. Especially one from America."

"Can I, Grandfather? Can I, can I?"

"She'll be all right?" asked Kramer, sounding worried.

"She'll be fine. The safety and happiness of children is why we exist, Mr. Kramer. As you will soon discover."

Newton took the young girl by the hand. "You come with me, Miss Penny. Your grandfather and Mr. Taine are expected inside. We'll leave them to their dull meeting. I will escort you to the tea."

Kramer watched the two figures walk down the road until they passed out of sight. Only then did he turn to his companion. "Who are these people, Taine? What did Newton mean?"

"I think I know. But why guess when we can find out the truth first hand. Let's go in. Obviously, they're waiting for us."

5.

The chapel was old, a thousand years or more. The bare stone walls dripped age. The ancient stone floor was worn flat by the passage of innumerable feet walking across its surface. The weight of the years hung in the air like a thick fog, discouraging small talk. Silently, Taine and Kramer walked through a short hallway to a pair of massive oak doors. Pushing them open, they found themselves in a large meeting room. Waiting for them, sitting behind a massive wood table, sat The Children of May.

They were dressed in simple, brown, woven-cloth robes. Three very ordinary men and three very ordinary women; none of them were smiling, nor did they look somber. If anything, Taine thought, The Children appeared expectant. In front of the six figures, resting on a dark velvet cloth, was an immense sheathed sword. Without asking, Taine knew its name.

"Gentlemen," said one of the women, rising from her chair. "Welcome. My name is Mary McCoy. Though all members of the council are equal, I have been chosen by my fellows to speak."

"Thank you," said Taine. Kramer remained silent, his gaze fixed on Excalibur. "We appreciate you agreeing to see us."

"We believe in helping those in need. Rich or poor, it matters not at all to The Children of May. We exist only to serve the helpless."

"It is real?" asked Wilson Kramer, his voice a whisper, filled with almost a religious awe.

"Yes, it is truly Excalibur. The sword of Arthur. We were given it by Elaine, Lady of the Lake." Then, with a flash of insight born of great wisdom, she added, "As we were given the scabbard holding it. That too, was rescued from the lake into which it was thrown by a servant of Morgan le Fay. Together, the two have rested here for over a thousand years."

In a daze, Kramer stepped forward. None of The Children said a word nor made any effort to stop him. Reaching down, he touched not the sword but the scabbard. Exactly as Taine expected. It was the sword's sheath that mattered to the millionaire.

"According to the legend," said Kramer, running his hands up and down the jewel-encrusted length of the scabbard, "as long as Arthur wore this scabbard, no wound could harm him. Its magic protected his blood. Only after it was stolen by Morgan le Fay was the king vulnerable."

"The scabbard is old," said Mary McCoy, "incredibly ancient. As is the blade whose true name is Caliburn. They were forged by the faerie smith, Wayland, long before men rose to power in this land. Created with a knowledge long forgotten, the sword was always intended to be the blade of heroes. Using it, Arthur united England, performing many great and noble deeds."

"And one truly terrible one," said Taine.

Mary McCoy nodded. "The king tried to cheat destiny. Unknowingly, Arthur slept with his sister, Morgan le Fay, and she bore him a son, Mordred. Still, it was a sin of the flesh, not of the spirit. For that, the king could have earned forgiveness."

"Not for the one that followed."

Again, Mary nodded, a look of infinite sadness clouding her features. "Arthur's bane was born on the first of May. That much Merlin knew through his magic. Thus, the magician told Arthur to summon all the children of high birth in the kingdom born on that day. Hundreds came, ranging in age from a few weeks to ten years. Like Pharaoh, like Herod, the king sought to alter fate through the murder of innocents. He could have disobeyed Merlin's command, but he did not. The king ordered the helpless children put to sea in a boat without a crew. Though he could not bear to kill them with his own hand, he condemned them to certain death."

"Mallory said the boat crashed into a cliff beneath a castle," said Taine, "with only Mordred surviving."

"The ship smashed to bits on the rocks. But six other survivors reached shore. Three boys and three girls, they thought of themselves as The Children of May. A half-dozen children, they lived their lives in secret, raised by Elaine, Lady of the Lake."

"And you are descended of those six?" asked Taine, fascinated by a tale never before told.

"The spiritual descendants," said Mary, smiling. "The council of The Children of May consists always of six members. When one dies, another is chosen from the ranks of those who were raised by the Order. That way, the lineage back to the original founders remains spiritually unbroken."

"I don't understand," said Kramer, his gaze sweeping along the table before coming to rest on Mary McCoy. "What is the purpose of your organization? What do you do?"

"Those six, the ones who survived the king's order, swore an oath as they grew older." Mary's face was solemn. "They dedicated their lives and the lives of all those who followed them to a sacred trust. As best they could, they would aid those children others refused to protect. They would stand for those who could not defend themselves. They would help the helpless, shelter the homeless, feed the hungry."

"And for a thousand years," said Taine, "you've continued that task."

"Exactly," said Mary. "The first six spent all their lives, aided by Elaine, establishing their order. They worked in secret, afraid that if Arthur learned they still lived, he would seek them out and destroy them. After his passing, they saw no reason to emerge from the shadows. Especially when the Lady of the Lake gave to their keeping the enchanted sword, Excalibur, and its magic scabbard."

"Why?" asked Kramer. "Why did she give them the sword?"

"For two reasons," said Mary. She paused for an instant, before continuing. "Most important, it served The Children as a symbol, a constant reminder, of the covenant they had made with themselves and their God."

Taine noted Mary did not reveal the second reason. He wondered why.

"The tenets of The Children of May were simple. They served the abandoned, the hopeless, the unprotected. At first, these were the orphans of war and disaster. That changed as the world changed. But the basic goals remained the same.

"Now we help primarily abused children and runaways. There are so many, and we can aid only a small handful. Still, we try our best. As well, we provide aid to other organizations throughout the world with the same goals."

"But the cost?" said Wilson Kramer. "The money needed to run an organization this size must be enormous."

"Early funding came from the noble parents of the original six. Later, those who were raised in safety donated their time and money. It has become a tradition among our charges. They feel an obligation to pay back what they are given. It is from their ranks that new members of the council are chosen. Who better to understand the problems of our children than those who suffered? Many others, like Miss Lawrence, find similar work elsewhere. Thus, the Order continues."

"My granddaughter, Penelope," said Kramer, his voice little more than a whisper. "She suffers from AIDS. The fatal accident that claimed the lives of my daughter and her husband, the negligence of the hospital, the attempted cover-up; all that doesn't matter. What is important is that she is fated to die before ever having a chance to live. Can the scabbard help her? Will you help her?"

Mary McCoy nodded. "Yes, to both questions. We deny charity to no child, rich or poor. But please understand that the magic of the scabbard can only do so much. Touching it will cleanse her blood of the disease for a week. No longer. For her to remain alive, she will have to stay here. Permanently, or until a cure is discovered. Can you bear giving her up?"

The millionaire's face froze in an emotionless mask. "I am a lonely old man. She's the only one I have. Her presence lights up my life. It'll be difficult, extremely difficult, without her. Yet, I must let her go." He nodded. "She can remain here."

"We shall make the necessary arrangements," said Mary McCoy. "Officially, Penny will be listed as a student attending our boarding school. While adults other than members of the Order are forbidden to stay on the grounds, as her only living relative, you can visit her. Often."

"That I shall. And your group can count on my financial support, my substantial support, from this day forward."

Taine knew he would accept no fee from the millionaire, not when the money could be better spent here. Besides, the chance to actually see Excalibur was payment enough.

"Thank you. The money will be put to good use. Still, we would have taken Penny even if you had not a dollar to your name."

"I know that. You are good people," said Kramer. "Truly, good people."

"We ask only that you do not reveal our secrets. If the world learns of the power of the scabbard, we will be overwhelmed. It's difficult turning away anyone in need. Yet we realize we can only help a few."

"No one will learn anything from me," said Kramer.

"Nor me," said Taine.

Mary McCoy smiled. "I expected no less. Mr. Taine, before the two of you leave, perhaps you will care to examine the sword? Even hold it in your hand? We here know of your interests in such mystic objects."

Taine stared at Excalibur's hilt. He had been caught completely off-guard by the suggestion. "You don't mind?"

"We wouldn't offer if we did."

Walking over to the huge broadsword, Taine placed his right hand on the hilt and pulled. The sword seemed to leap out of the scabbard, and without effort he raised Excalibur up into the air. A glow of white light filled the room. The blade blazed like a beacon. Holding it, Taine felt himself filled with a nobility of purpose, a purity of spirit that touched the very essence of his being. Looking around at the others, he could see from their faces that the sword's aura affected them similarly. The force of the blade was overwhelming.

Ancient runes, written in no human tongue, covered one side of the blade. Somehow, staring at them, Taine knew they said, *Take Me.*

"Turn the sword over," said Mary McCoy.

Taine did so and stared at an inscription in modern-day English. *Cast me away!*

His will not his own, the detective replaced the sword back in its scabbard. Immediately as Excalibur was sheathed, he felt the effect of its glow depart.

"Only by experiencing Wayland's spell can you under-stand the second reason that the faerie queen, Elaine, gave us the blade," said Mary McCoy. She spoke quietly, slowly, but in tones that Taine would never forget. It was as if the Lady of the Lake spoke across the ages directly to all those in the chamber. "It is a lesson that most men have yet to learn.

"When you think of the magic of Excalibur," she declared, "remember The Children of May. Never forget the hundreds of innocent children sacrificed by the high-born king who held that same blade, felt that same force. Be thus ever reminded of the terrible evil deeds noble men are willing to perform in the name of good.

"That is the true legacy of the great sword of King Arthur. That and no other."

ABOUT THE AUTHOR

Bob Weinberg was born in Newark, New Jersey on August 29th, 1946. In fifth grade, he read "The Devil and Daniel Webster," by Stephen Vincent Benet, and knew beyond any shadow of a doubt that he wanted to become a writer. It's a dream he's followed since.

During the past 47 years, Bob has written and sold nearly 100 short stories, 16 novels, 17 non-fiction books and more than two dozen comic book scripts. He's edited more than 150 anthologies and short story collections. Bob's work has been published in 20 countries and 15 languages.

He's won 2 Bram Stoker Awards, given by the Horror Writers Association; 2 World Fantasy Awards; and 2 Society of Technical Writers Awards. He served 2 terms as Vice President of the Horror Writers Association. He's the only person in the history of the organization to win the group's Silver Hammer Award for service to the association 2 times.

Bob has also been a member of the Board of Trustees for the World Fantasy Convention for the past 24 years.

Despite all his success, Bob Weinberg is not yet ready to retire. He's still looking to write the perfect story. He's intent on composing a story that resonates with his readers the way "The Devil and Daniel Webster" did with him. It's a goal he may never achieve, but he intends to keep trying.

Something to build upon

A GRAPHIC NOVEL BY TIM BRODERICK

David Diangelo is a high-tech drifter with a talent for keeping secrets and fixing problems that are too sensitive, or too personal, for the police. He's not afraid to operate outside the law when murder, paternity and betrayal are the stakes – especially when his life is on the line!

Twilight Tales is proud to present for the first time ever in printed form, this fine graphic novel which originally debuted on the web as a very popular series, garnering rave reviews.

Also, don't miss the *Lost Child* storyline from Tim's Odd Jobs web comic available on the Twilight Tales website at www.TwilightTales.com.

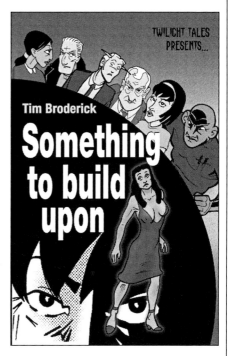

"An instant crime classic. Diangelo is one plugged-in, jacked-up Dilbert, a high plains drifter of the Internet, world-weary computer in occasional gumshoes."
– **Kevin Burton Smith**, Editor, Thrilling Detective website

"An intriguing tale that pushes the boundaries of the graphic novel."
– **Raymond Benson**
Estate-authorized author of the James Bond novels and author of *Evil Hours*

"Tim Broderick's *Something to build upon* is something to be proud of. Well-drawn, distinctive characters in a solid plot and a real sense of urban angst. These are people you can care about."
– **Barbara D'Amato**, Author of the best-selling *Cat Marsala* mysteries

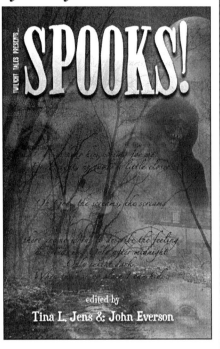

THE CRAWLING ABATTOIR
EXPANDED EDITION
BY MARTIN MUNDT

Featuring 13 stories of humorously twisted horror from the amazing mind of Martin Mundt.

"The work of newcomer Martin Mundt is sick, insane, surreal, and thoroughly enjoyable. I'm looking forward to more."
– F. Paul Wilson, author of *The Keep* and *Deep As The Marrow*

"Strange, silly, funny tales in extremely poor taste. Highly recommended - also recommended for those who are high."
– Poppy Z. Brite author of *Lost Souls* and *The Crow: Lazarus Heart*

"Nazi dragons, lethal llamas, full-body zippers, Pierced Pets... all this and Kevin Bacon too! Sort of. If Mundt doesn't make you smile you're probably as dead and immune to black humor as his cherished Celebrity Corpse."
– Jack Ketchum, author of *The Girl Next Door* and *Stranglehold*

"Martin Mundt is a nasty, warped, zero-temperature so-and-so who can't put two words together without first snickering, then slitting their throats. No wonder reading him is such a pleasure."
– Peter Straub author of *Floating Dragon* and *Hellfire Club*

Vigilantes of Love

BY JOHN EVERSON

This single-author collection by the Bram Stoker award-winning author of the novel *Covenant* offers 15 tales colored by the ambient music of zombies, witches, vampires, ghosts and even a soul-thirsty moon.

"John Everson has a flair for starting a story down one path and then just when we know where it is going and how it will end, he turns it around and reminds us that life is unpredictable. *Vigilantes of Love* is a collection of 15 well-written stories that range from fantasy to horror. Some are hardcore horror stories and some are lighter fare. All of them are worth reading....

It is hard to pick a favorite tale from these stories because I enjoyed them all. Whenever I thought that a particular story was my favorite I would be drawn to another title and then another. Each one vying for the top spot.

One of the better collections I have read in some time. I give it 5 bookwyrms."
– **Jimmy Z**, *FeoAmante.com*

"John Everson is a renaissance man, talented in so many fields including the composing of horror. I say composing, as he creates it much as he does his music, with attention to perfect details that resonate through all the senses. He is going to be even more amazing than he already is."
– **Charlee Jacob**, author of *Haunter*

"His stories are an exhilarating mix of brains and horrific brawn – scary, controversial, and unforgettable. Everson manages to tackle a variety of story scapes and stylistic modes, and he brings them all off with a crackling effectiveness."
– **Edward Lee**, author of *City Infernal* and *Infernal Angel*

The Undertow of Small Town Dreams

BY JOHN WEAGLY

This collection by John Weagly chronicles the legends and lives of Currie Valley – a hazy little town on the banks of the Mighty Mississippi. It's a quiet place, filled with ex-wrestlers, a bandit dreaming of glory and fame, a mistreated werewolf and love in a meteor shower. In Currie Valley, as with any good undertow, you might just get carried away.

"I love pleasant surprises and, in this business, one of the best pleasant surprises is finding evidence of a new writer worth reading and following. Thus I wish to bring to your attention a slender but handsomely produced collection of short stories called, evocatively enough, *The Undertow of Small Town Dreams*, by John Weagly...

"By the evidence presented in the 14 brief stories, he's an emerging writer of some accomplished work, and even more highly promising fiction looming on the near horizon....The tonal keys to Weagly's stories are whimsy and both the light and dark fantastic. There's a sense of Midwestern tall tale at work, along with a dash of the unexpectedly surreal. When the stories work to full advantage, they overcome what at first appears to be sheer insubstantiality. The effect can be pleasingly delayed, a ticking time bomb to disturb the reader's thoughts long after setting the book down....Weird, but affecting.

"That last is a phrase that applies to much of *The Undertow of Small Town Dreams*. As I indicated earlier, John Weagly is definitely a writer to watch..."

—Edward Bryant, *Locus Magazine*